fake
boyfriend

by
KATE BRIAN

2/08

SIMON & SCHUSTER BOOKS FOR YOUNG READERS

New York   London   Toronto   Sydney

SIMON & SCHUSTER BOOKS FOR YOUNG READERS
An imprint of Simon & Schuster Children's Publishing Division
1230 Avenue of the Americas, New York, NY 10020

Produced by Alloy Entertainment
151 West 26th Street
New York, NY 10001

Book design by Andrea C. Uva
The text of this book is set in Minion.
Manufactured in the United States of America
2 4 6 8 10 9 7 5 3 1
Library of Congress Cataloging-in-Publication Data
Brian, Kate, 1974–
Fake boyfriend / Kate Brian. — 1st ed.
p. cm.
Summary: When Lane and Vivi's best friend Isabelle has her heart
broken by her unreliable boyfriend, they decide to save her by inventing
a new boy on the internet to ask Isabelle to the prom, but the scheme
quickly becomes complicated, and the results surprise them all.
ISBN-13: 978-1-4169-1367-2   ISBN-10: 1-4169-1367-X
[1. Interpersonal relations—Fiction. 2. Dating (Social customs)—Fiction.
3. Mistaken identity—Fiction. 4. High schools—Fiction. 5. Schools—Fiction.
6. Friendship—Fiction.] I. Title.
PZ7.B75875Fak 2007   [Fic]—dc22   2007024328

FIRST
EDITION

For Matt, my forever boyfriend

★ ★ ★ ★ *one* ★ ★ ★ ★

"Who would *ever* buy something like that?" Vivi Swayne grabbed the *Lucky* magazine her friend Lane Morris was holding. It was open to a page full of hideous black-and-white dresses that looked like they'd walked out of an *Alice in Wonderland* nightmare—all checkerboard patterns and ridiculously poufy skirts. It was only one month until their prom, and neither of them had a dress yet. But if this was the junk the fashion world was offering, Vivi thought she might be better off without one. "I wouldn't even wear one of those on a dare."

"Please. You've never taken a dare in your life," Lane pointed out, leaning back in the green vinyl booth at Lonnie's Bagels and Coffee Shop, sipping her chai. All around them, groups of kids from Westmont High chatted, sipped their coffees, and noshed on Lonnie's famous chocolate desserts. The brightly lit family-owned place was all chrome accents, fluorescent lights, and old-school counters and booths, yet somehow it managed to maintain a cozy appeal. During the morning rush it catered to frenzied commuters and their caffeine addictions before they hopped the train to New York City. During lunch it was *the* local destination for deli sandwiches. But in the evening it was a favorite hangout for the Westmont High population, and it had enough designer coffees and sweets on the menu to keep their sugar rushes rushing all night long.

"It's true," Curtis Miles added from across the table, gesturing with a decadent-looking forkful of chocolate cake.

Lane blushed fiercely under her freckles and pulled her long red hair over her shoulder so she could busy herself with tugging at it. Vivi had come to recognize it as a nervous gesture—one that was most often inspired by Curtis. Even though the two of them had been neighbors since they were on tricycles, Lane had been harboring a huge crush on Curtis for the past couple of years. Curtis, however, was totally and completely clueless that he inspired it.

"I've taken a dare!" Vivi protested, snatching the fork from Curtis's hand. She took a huge bite of the cake and pushed the plate back across the table. "What about the time I ate that entire carton of Chubby Hubby in ten minutes?"

"Yeah, but you wanted to do that anyway," Lane said.

Vivi deflated slightly. "Okay, fine. So I don't like it when other people tell me what to do. That's not news." Vivi pulled her long legs up underneath her on the bench. She tossed the mag aside and picked up her black-and-white cookie, taking a bite out of the white side. Slumping down, she settled back next to Lane and moved her head around until she found a comfortable position—one that kept the rubber band holding her thick blond ponytail from jabbing into the back of her head. "Where the hell is Isabelle already?" Isabelle and Vivi had been best friends since they shared a desk pod together in first grade, and when they met Lane and Curtis in middle school, the four melded together in a perfect little foursome. Even though Curtis didn't always chill with them now, they were still all really close and had promised Izzy they would meet to talk about prom, since, naturally, they were all going together. "You told her Lonnie's, right? Not Starbucks?"

"Why would we tell her Starbucks? We never go to Starbucks. It's evil," Curtis said, glaring out the window at the new shop that had gone up across the street last winter.

"Please. You're addicted to their Frappuccinos," Vivi scoffed.

"They do make a mean Frappuccino," Curtis agreed, staring into his plain coffee.

"Curtis! God!" Vivi whacked his arm. "Lonnie's right *there*."

They all glanced over at the elderly proprietor behind the counter, who seemed to live in her shop. She was currently counting out change for Kim Wolfe, one of their classmates. Normally loud and totally obnoxious, Kim waited patiently, snapping her gum, as Lonnie sifted out her pennies one by one. Everyone was patient for Lonnie. The woman was an institution.

"It's not like she can hear us," Lane said, lowering her voice.

"She turns her hearing aid down when the place is this

JP'd" Curtis added, shoving his long brown bangs away from his big brown eyes.

"JP'd?" Vivi asked impatiently.

"Jam-packed," Curtis said with a shrug.

"Okay, the whole initializing everything is getting beyond annoying," Vivi told him.

"Tell me how you really feel," Curtis shot back, smoothing his bangs back again.

Just then, the front door opened and in walked their significant fourth, Isabelle Hunter. Tonight, Izzy looked as perfect as ever in a pink turtleneck sweater, skinny jeans, and black ankle boots. Her cocoa-colored skin was blemish-free, her straight hair pulled back in a white headband, and tiny diamonds sparkled in her ears.

"Omigod! You guys are so gonna love me!" Isabelle squealed, rushing over to their table. She slapped a pink binder down on the table with the word PROM spelled across the cover in big glitter letters.

"Uh, you really sure you want to bring that thing out in public?" Vivi asked as Izzy scooted in next to Curtis. It was Isabelle's infamous Prom Planner, which she'd been working on since ninth grade.

"Uh, yeah, I do. Since it has inside . . ." Isabelle rifled through the many colorful, dog-eared pages filled with dresses, flowers, limos, jewelry, shoes, bags, and other random photos she'd cut out of magazines over the years, and she yanked out a yellow sheet from the back. "Ta-da!" she announced, holding it up with a huge grin. "One receipt for a white Mercedes stretch limo!"

"What!?" Vivi gasped, grabbing the page.

"I booked it this afternoon. It's perfect and it's all ours," Isabelle said giddily. "It fits four couples, so we're all in!"

"Iz, this is so OTH!" Curtis said.

"Off the hook?" Isabelle guessed.

Vivi saw the rental fee total at the bottom of the page and whistled under her breath. "Uh, Iz? This is, like, Mount Everest steep."

"It's already paid for," Isabelle said, waving a hand. "I got graduation money from my grandparents, and it was about four times as much as I thought it was going to be."

"You're kidding," Lane said. Isabelle's grandfather, a former NBA superstar, was always bestowing insane gifts on his grandkids. "Isabelle, that's incredible."

"In that case, wanna pay for my tux, too?" Curtis joked, gulping down his coffee.

"Why not? I paid for Shawn's," Isabelle said, grabbing Lane's unused fork and digging into Curtis's cake.

Lane, Vivi, and Curtis exchanged a look of doom. "You didn't," Vivi said.

Isabelle shrugged. "This is what people do when they're in a mature relationship, Vivi," she replied, taking on the tone of a kindergarten teacher.

"Yeah, or when they're in a relationship where one person is totally taking advantage of the other," Vivi muttered. A comment that Isabelle ignored, as usual.

Vivi, however, was officially irritated. Isabelle was valedictorian of their class, captain of the girls' varsity basketball team; she never drank, smoked, or cursed, and had recently received a commendation from the mayor of their small New Jersey town for her volunteer work with Meals on Wheels. She'd been accepted early admission to Stanford University. She was the class's crown jewel. Her boyfriend, Shawn Littig, however, was the class screwup. Shawn was constantly rolling in late, cutting class to sneak cigarettes, and talking back to teachers just to show that he could. Everyone knew he was a total jerk, but Isabelle maintained that he was just misunderstood and that no one knew Shawn the way she did. Unfortunately, Vivi had a feeling it was the other way around: Everyone in the world could read Shawn Littig like a book—a seriously trashy, bargain-bin novel, to be exact—but he had Isabelle completely and totally snowed.

"He just spent all that money on his car, so he was totally tapped out," Isabelle explained. "And my date is not going to prom in jeans and a T-shirt."

"Well, he should have saved. Everyone knows how important prom is to you," Vivi said. "Or is he the only one who's never been taken on a page-by-page tour of that?" she asked, nodding at the prom book.

"Hey. Do not dis the book," Isabelle scolded, placing a protective hand on the cover. "And yes, he has seen it. In fact, he got the exact tuxedo I picked out for him from the sophomore year *Teen Vogue* prom issue," she added proudly. "Speaking of which, has Jeffrey rented his tux yet?"

Vivi took a deep breath. She had been hoping to avoid this conversation, but she should have known better. "Um . . . Jeffrey and I kind of broke up." Vivi picked at a random crusty stain on the green vinyl.

"What? When?" Isabelle demanded.

"Did you know?" Lane asked Curtis, reaching across the table to smack his arm.

"Uh . . . I talked to Jeff this morning," Curtis replied, rubbing his arm and looking snagged.

"Why didn't you tell me?" Lane demanded.

"Hello, I'm a guy. We have a code." Curtis rolled his eyes.

"Vivi, what happened?" Isabelle interrupted. "I thought—"

Vivi held up her hands, and her friends all fell silent. "We broke up last night. No big. It had to happen eventually."

She cracked off the black half of her cookie, folded it, and shoved the whole thing into her mouth, looking out the window in hopes of putting a quick end to the subject. Across the street, Starbucks was overflowing with freshmen and sophomores who weren't cool enough yet to get the understated allure of Lonnie's.

"Vivi, what happened? Why didn't you call?" Lane asked.

"Are you okay?" Isabelle put in.

"I'm fine," Vivi said through her mouthful of cookie. "We only went out for, like, three weeks. It's not the end of the world."

It wasn't like she could actually tell them the truth. Jeffrey had told her he liked her, but said that it was pretty clear that she didn't actually like him. Every guy Vivi had ever gone out with since middle school had said pretty much the same thing—or some variation of it.

"He broke up with you, didn't he?" Lane said softly. Then, when Vivi didn't answer, she groaned. "Viv, I told you that if you kept picking on him like that—"

Vivi sighed. They had had this conversation ten million times before. Daniel Lin had been Vivi's eighth-grade boyfriend. They had gone out for months, and Vivi had been crazy for him. He was smart, funny, hot, athletic, and totally attentive for an eighth-grade boy. Everything she could ever have imagined wanting in a boyfriend. And then, out of nowhere, he'd broken up with her for another girl, and Vivi had been crushed. But she had gotten over it and Daniel had moved away and that was that. Vivi thought it was mildly ridiculous that her friends thought that this one thing affected every relationship she'd had since. Vivi never even thought about Daniel except when Lane and Izzy brought him up. Well, almost never.

"Can we *please* change the subject?" Vivi asked, staring out the window again. Instantly, her heart dropped and she dropped her cookie. She could not be seeing what she was seeing. No way. No . . . freaking . . . way. She kicked Curtis under the table and nodded toward Starbucks.

Curtis looked out the window, and his eyes grew wide. "Oh my God," he said.

"What?" Isabelle asked, looking over.

"Isabelle! Don't!" Vivi said automatically. Vivi thought she was going to hyperventilate. Shawn Littig, the guy Isabelle had been dating on and off since freshman year, the guy she was so in love with that she was somehow blinded to the fact he was a total sleezeball, had just walked out of Starbucks with his arm around Tricia Blank—a sophomore who took her imitation of trashy celebutante fashion way too far. And now, he was pressing her up against the brick wall of the building, shoving his tongue so far down her throat, she was gonna need the Heimlich.

And Izzy had seen the whole thing. Her face paled, and she made a choking sound in the back of her throat.

"Oh my God," Lane said, finally catching on. She looked fretfully at Isabelle. "Iz, it's—"

"No. No, no, no, no, no, no, no," Isabelle rambled.

She shoved herself out of the booth and ran outside. For a split second, Vivi was too stunned to move. Then, she, Lane, and Curtis all jumped up and followed. Isabelle stormed to the corner, where the evening traffic was lazily making its way down the road.

"Shawn!" Isabelle yelled at the top of her lungs.

Across the street, Shawn sprang away from Tricia. Isabelle quickly looked both ways, somehow judged that the oncoming Jeep Wrangler was not going to hit her, and dived into the street.

"Isabelle!" Vivi screeched, shoving her hands into the pockets of her green zip-up and running after her friend.

Curtis ran out ahead of Vivi and threw his hands up to stop traffic. The Jeep slammed on its brakes and squealed to a stop.

"What the hell are you doing?" the driver shouted.

"Sorry! Crisis in the making here," Curtis said. He waved Vivi and Lane across the street, then quickly followed.

"What are you doing!?" Isabelle cried as all the kids on the sidewalk stopped to stare.

Shawn backed away from Tricia as if she were on fire and gaped at Isabelle. His light blue eyes darted around as if looking for an escape route. Vivi only hoped he would try to get past her. That way she could punch him right in his infuriatingly hot face.

"Isabelle!" Shawn said, stunned.

"Oh, please. Half the school is here," Vivi blurted, her hands curled into fists. "Did you really think you wouldn't get caught?"

"Back off," Shawn snapped at Vivi. "This is none of your business."

Vivi gritted her teeth and fumed.

"What's going on?" Isabelle asked shakily.

Shawn looked imploringly at Isabelle. "Baby . . . can we just go someplace and talk . . . on our own?"

"Hey!" Tricia protested, crossing her skinny arms over her barely-there tank top. "You told me you broke up with her."

Vivi's heart plummeted as Izzy's eyes filled with tears. "What? Shawn . . . you're breaking up with me?"

Shawn glanced around and seemed to realize there was no way out of this. He looked at the ground, his dark hair falling over his face, and shook his head. "I'm sorry, Iz . . . I'm with Tricia now."

"With her? *With* her?" Isabelle blurted. "For how long?"

"About a month," Tricia said smugly, sliding her arm around Shawn's waist and snuggling into his side.

"The last—" Isabelle buckled slightly, as if she'd been kicked in the knees. All the air went right out of Vivi's lungs. She stepped over and put her arm around Izzy. Her friend started convulsing, tears streaming down her face.

"Iz, please . . . ," Shawn said, extricating himself from Tricia's grasp. "I didn't mean to hurt you. I—"

Vivi glared up at Shawn. "Walk away. Right now," she said through her teeth.

Shawn snorted a laugh. "You can't tell me what to do."

"I think we just did," Curtis said, stepping up between Shawn and the girls and getting right in Shawn's face.

Shawn had four inches and approximately twenty pounds on Curtis, but he was showing no fear. Shawn raised his hands and backed off. Coward. Vivi knew he welcomed the excuse to bail, not to have to deal. Just like all the other times he'd broken up with Izzy—via note, e-mail, text, a message on her voice mail. It was always in the most cowardly way possible. And yet, Isabelle always took him back. Every time. No matter what.

Well, maybe that was all about to change. Izzy couldn't forgive him this time. This time he'd *actually* cheated on her. And half the school had witnessed it.

"Isabelle, are you okay?" Lane asked as Shawn and Tricia headed for his vintage Vette, parked down the street.

"He's been cheating on me for a month!" Isabelle blurted, hugging Lane and clinging to her light blue sweater. "A month! How is that even possible?"

"I know, Iz. I'm sorry," Lane said, stroking her hair.

Vivi glanced around at the freshmen and sophomores, who were still looking on quietly, eavesdropping as hard as they could. Vivi glared around at the onlookers and gently pulled Izzy away and back toward the street.

"And with Tricia Blank!" Isabelle ranted. "She's a . . . a . . ."

Skank? Cheesebomb? Easy McSlutty? Vivi thought.

". . . sophomore!" Isabelle wailed.

Lane frowned sympathetically. "We know, Iz."

"It's gonna be okay." Vivi put her hand on her friend's back. Her heart felt sick. Worse than it had when Jeffrey had dumped her last night. This was Isabelle. Her best friend since grade school. Izzy's heartache had more of an effect on Vivi than her own did. "Come on. Let's get out of here," Vivi said.

"I'll go get our stuff and meet up with you guys," Curtis said, jogging over to Lonnie's.

"We'll go back to my house and . . . I don't know . . . come up with a revenge plan," Vivi said comfortingly. "Between us we should definitely be able to whip up a voodoo doll," she joked, trying to lighten the mood.

Isabelle choked a laugh and nodded through a fresh wave of tears. "Okay." Vivi had a feeling the girl would agree to anything right then.

"Don't worry, Iz," Lane said as they headed down the street toward the municipal parking lot and Vivi's car. "Everything's gonna be okay."

"Yeah, it is, because if the voodoo doll doesn't work, I'm going to go over there and kick his ass. Believe me," Vivi said, determined. "That idiot has broken your heart for the last time."

★ ★ ★ ★ *two* ★ ★ ★ ★

Pick up tray with both hands. Place change on tray. Do not drop change. Do not . . . drop . . .

Lane managed to transfer the coins and bills from her sweaty palm onto the side of her plastic lunch tray without overturning the whole thing. She breathed a sigh of relief and smiled in triumph at the cafeteria worker. The woman looked like she was about to phone the school shrink.

Lane managed an apologetic smile and stepped aside.

"And then, out of nowhere, my dad's like, 'If you don't get all A's and B's on your final report card, you're not going to camp,'" Curtis babbled to her as he stepped up to the register. "I mean, how wrong is that? I'm a head counselor this year."

As always, he was totally oblivious of Lane's extreme stress—all of which was caused by him. Lane pretty much lived not to do anything embarrassing in front of Curtis. As long as she didn't, she figured that one day her fantasy of

13

him waking up and realizing she was his one true love might actually come true. She knew it was a thin thread of logic, but she had to cling to something.

"Don't you think?" Curtis asked.

"What? Oh yeah," Lane replied, not really knowing what she was agreeing to.

"So then I'm, like, I am so totally screwed. I mean, there's no way I can pull a B in Calc. Lazinsky sucks, giving us that much homework," Curtis continued. He paid for his lunch, pocketed the change, and picked up his tray with one hand. He clearly had no problem. "We're graduating in a month. Is he some kind of sadist?"

"You could just not do it," Lane suggested.

"Were you not listening to me? I have to get a B or no camp this summer. I have to do it," Curtis told her as they started down the center aisle of the cafeteria. Lane glanced at him from the corner of her eye and smiled. As silly as it was, she loved the way he looked in this light. The gold flecks in his brown eyes seemed brighter, and the sun brought out the red highlights in his floppy brown hair. What she wouldn't give to be able to paint him in the middle of the cafeteria. It would totally be her masterpiece. The best thing she'd done all year, hands down. If only she could get him to . . .

"So will you?"

Lane stopped walking abruptly, and her soda almost slid off the edge of her tray. Luckily, Curtis caught it in time.

"Whoops. That was close," he said with a grin. There was the tiniest little chip in his front tooth from a skateboarding accident he'd had earlier that year. He always touched his tongue to it when he was concentrating really hard. It was totally adorable.

"Will I what?" Lane asked, balancing the tray against her hip. She nervously pulled her hair over her shoulder.

"Help me. With Calc. After school," Curtis said in a voice that made it perfectly clear he'd said all of it already.

Lane had planned on spending her afternoon in the art studio finishing up her senior project. She'd been looking forward to it, actually. She had even created a new playlist on her iPod for inspiration. But Curtis was looking at her with big, puppy dog eyes, and she could never turn down that face.

"Sure. Want to meet up in the library after eighth?" she said, tugging at her hair again.

Curtis grinned. "What would I do without you?"

I don't know. But right now you should kiss me, she thought. Then she blushed and turned around, heading for their prime cafeteria spot.

They always sat in the same place, right next to the glass doors to the courtyard, which were always open on a beautiful spring day like this one, letting in the warm sweet-smelling air. Lane's knees were quaking a bit after her space-out, and she couldn't have been more relieved when she slid safely into a chair. Unfortunately, the vibe at the table was not a happy one. Isabelle was slumped in her seat as she had been all week, listlessly toying with her fork, while Vivi eyed her sadly. This had to stop. Lane had never seen her friend so depressed for so many days in a row. Usually, she and Shawn would have kissed and made up by now—not that Lane wanted *that* to happen. She just wished she could figure out some other way to cheer Isabelle up.

"Hi, guys!" Lane said brightly.

"Hey." Isabelle's voice was barely a whisper.

"What's up?" Curtis asked, shaking his chocolate milk. He looked around at the girls hopefully, as he'd been doing all week long. Lane knew he was just waiting for them all to snap out of it already. Curtis was a good friend to them, but he knew nothing about the required female mourning period after the end of an intense relationship.

"Nothing," Isabelle replied in another near whisper, staring listlessly out the window.

Curtis sighed, shrugged, and grabbed a fry. Lane saw him look at Isabelle out of the corner of his eye, and she knew he was trying to think of a way to cheer her up. Which only made her love him more.

The door to the cafeteria opened, and Lane and Vivi both looked up automatically, as anyone facing the door did when there was a latecomer. It was Tricia Blank, and she was wearing a very familiar black sweater. Lane's face prickled with heat, and she looked over at Vivi. Instantly she knew Vivi recognized it, too. They had, after all, spent an hour in the hot, crowded, Christmastime mall helping Isabelle pick it out. And another half an hour helping her select the perfect manly wrapping paper for it.

"Oh, I don't believe this . . . ," Vivi snarled through gritted teeth.

"What?" Isabelle asked, turning around. Lane wouldn't have thought it possible, but Izzy's skin actually grew sallower before her eyes. "Wait. Is that the—?"

"The sweater you bought Shawn for Christmas?" Vivi fumed, shaking her head.

Isabelle looked over at Shawn's table, where he sat with the rest of his friends—kids who thought that wearing offensive T-shirts and keeping packs of cigarettes in the back pockets of their jeans made them anarchists. Shawn instantly locked eyes with Isabelle, as if he had Izzy radar, then glanced over at Tricia, who was busy smiling and chatting with some of her girlfriends near the wall. He was out of his chair like a shot and walked right over to Isabelle's side.

"Belle," he said, his blue eyes pained.

"You gave her my sweater?" Isabelle said, her voice thick.

"No. I swear. She must have taken it out of my dresser," Shawn said pleadingly. As if he cared about Isabelle's feelings. As if he had any conscience at all.

"She was in your room?" Isabelle half whimpered.

Shawn pushed his hands into the front pockets of his jeans and looked around at the others. "Belle, can we please just talk for a second?"

"Don't call me Belle," Isabelle said sadly.

"Fine. I'm sorry. You're right. Can we just . . . please?"

"Fine," Isabelle said, standing.

She and Shawn walked to the other end of the table near the open doors.

"Unbelievable," Vivi said, shaking her head so furiously that her messy blond bun tumbled into a ponytail. "I can't believe she's actually talking to him."

She got up quietly and walked around the table, headed for the vending machines near the wall—about three feet from where Izzy and Shawn were now standing.

"Vivi!" Lane hissed.

Vivi turned around and shot her a wide-eyed look, telling her to shut up. Lane deflated and turned back to her food. It wasn't like she was going to argue. Vivi was going to do what Vivi wanted to do anyway.

Over at the vending machines, Vivi made a good show of it, pulling some change out of her pocket and pretending like she was totally baffled by the myriad candy choices. Meanwhile, Shawn and Izzy just kept talking, too engrossed in their conversation to notice the eavesdropper. Finally Vivi aggressively punched in a number, grabbed her Twix bar, and stormed back to the table. She yanked out her chair and dropped into it with a huff.

"Okay, that guy should be a politician," Vivi said. "He is all slime."

"Why? What's going on?" Curtis asked, finally buying into the soap opera.

"First of all, he said he still cares about her and always will," Vivi grumbled. "And that he'd never give the sweater she gave him to another girl."

"Well, that's good, right?" Curtis asked before chugging his milk.

Vivi rolled her eyes. "Then he told her that she should move on. That he thinks she's too good for him and she can do better," she whispered furiously.

Lane snorted. "Well, he's got that right."

"Yeah, but to him it's a total joke. He knew she was going to disagree, which of course she totally did. 'I don't understand why you're so hard on yourself. I love you. You know that,'" she said, doing a perfect imitation of Isabelle's voice. "He's totally keeping her hanging. I swear I could just—" She curled her hands into fists and grunted in frustration.

"Okay, okay. Calm down," Lane said, putting her hand over Vivi's.

"She can't take him back," Vivi said, shaking her head. "She can't be second to Tricia Skank-Ho Blank. We need to stage an intervention. Threaten her with something."

Lane rolled an empty straw wrapper in her fingers and laughed. "Like what?"

"I don't know . . . maybe we should tell her we won't be friends with her anymore! Freeze her out," Vivi announced. "Tough love, like in that DVD we watched in health class sophomore year."

"Um . . . Isabelle's not a crack addict," Lane pointed out.

"No. But she is a Shawn addict," Vivi shot back.

Lane's heart dropped. Vivi couldn't be serious. At least, Lane hoped she wasn't. Because usually, when Vivi came up with a plan, she stuck to it. And she made everyone around her stick to it as well.

"We can't do that," Curtis said, crumpling up the empty milk container. "It's way too mean. And besides, none of us could actually go through with it."

Vivi's face dropped and she slumped. "You're right. But we have to do something to make her realize she doesn't need this jerk," Vivi said, glancing over at them. Lane saw Isabelle nod at something Shawn was saying, and the very sight made her tense.

Lane shook her head. "Isabelle is *way* too good for him. If she goes back to him, it'll be a total disaster."

Curtis nodded, his mouth full.

"Good. At least we all see it," Vivi said, setting her jaw in a determined way. She pulled her sneaker-clad feet up on the chair and rested her chin on her knees. "Now we just have to come up with a way to make *her* see it."

"Do you really think empowerment-movie night is going to help?" Lane asked, sifting through the pile of DVDs Vivi had rented.

"It's just a preliminary plan. Until I come up with the real one," Vivi said, setting a huge bowl of popcorn down on the table in her basement.

The basement door opened. "Hi, honey! I'm home!" Vivi's mother trilled jokingly as she tromped down the stairs.

She was wearing one of her more colorful head scarves, with her curly blond hair sticking out in two perfect triangles on either side of her head from her ears to her shoulders. Huge wooden monstrosities dangled from her earlobes, and her makeup was even more elaborate than usual. As always, Vivi's mom had gone all-out for her work party that evening. It was one of the hazards of working at the regional theater, the Starlight Playhouse. There was, apparently, a lot of pressure to look as boho kooky as possible.

"I just thought you girls might want some snacks!" She lifted a grease-stained brown bag. "Leftovers from the cast party!"

"Oooh! I knew I loved you for a reason." Vivi grabbed the bag from her mother. Inside was a stack of white takeout plates with clear covers. Mini hot dogs, mini quiches, mini spring rolls. She tore off the lids and started laying the food out on the table.

"Hi, Ms. Swayne," Lane said, standing up. She walked around the table and hugged Vivi's mom.

"Hello, dear!" Vivi's mother exclaimed, high on life. "What are you girls doing? Movie night? Got anything good?" She inspected the array of films. "Oh! Kate Winslet? I just love her. The actress who starred in my production of *Twelfth Night* last month reminded me so much of her."

"Cool, Mom. And we'd love to hear all about it. Really. But Isabelle's gonna be here any second so . . ." Vivi advanced on her mother, steering her back toward the stairs.

"Oh. Okay. Well, if you girls need anything—"

"We won't," Vivi said, patting her mother on the back. "But thanks for the snacks."

Her mother's shoulders drooped, and her hundreds of plastic bracelets clicked together. "Okay. Well. I'll be upstairs."

"Bye!" Vivi smiled until her mother was gone, then turned around and rolled her eyes. She shoved her hands into the pockets of her oversized track hoodie and slumped down onto the couch.

"I don't know why you're so mean to her," Lane said with a sigh, munching on one of the mini hot dogs.

"Lane, you know that she'd stay down here all night if I didn't kick her out," Vivi said, grabbing a quiche from one of the plates. "She thinks she's one of us."

"Well, she's cooler than my mom," Lane said, pulling her long hair into a high ponytail.

Vivi laughed. "I'd give *anything* to have your mom."

Lane's mother worked as an image consultant at a huge media conglomerate in New York. She was stylish, sophisticated, and unmeddling. In other words, the exact opposite of drama queen Sylvia Swayne.

"Yeah, well, if I ever see her, I'll tell her you said that," Lane deadpanned.

The doorbell rang, and Vivi and Lane both jumped up. "Finally!"

"I got it!" Vivi shouted.

She barreled up the stairs with Lane on her heels and slid across the hallway in her socks. But when she got there, her younger brother, Marshall, was already talking to Isabelle, who was eyeing him uncertainly from the front step, as most people eyed Vivi's book-loving, pasty-faced brother. His blond hair was, as always, slicked back from his face with some thick gel, and he was wearing a T-shirt that read LOVE ME, LOVE MY MAC. Vivi wanted to groan just looking at him. The kid could have been somewhat cute and maybe halfway cool if he wasn't so intent on being a dork.

"I got it, loser," Vivi told him, hip-checking him out of the way.

"Shut up," Marshall grumbled, blushing slightly. "See you later, guys. I'll be in the living room," he told them.

"Don't care," Vivi shot back. Marshall narrowed his green eyes—exactly the same shade as Vivi's—and went.

"Bye, Marshall," Isabelle said, polite as ever.

She stepped inside, and Vivi closed the door. "Okay, what do you want to watch first? *The Holiday*? *She's the Man*? *Erin Brockovich*?"

"Iz?" Lane said uncertainly. "Are you all right?"

Vivi's heart clenched, and she turned around. Tears were streaming down Isabelle's face. She dropped her Kate Spade overnight bag on the floor and wailed, "He's going to the prom with her!"

"Omigod, Izzy!" Lane said. "How did you . . . Who told you?"

"She did! I ran into her at the mall, and she was all showing off about it!" Isabelle cried. "He's taking her to the prom in the tux I picked out. The one that I paid for!"

"What an asshole," Vivi said through her teeth. The prom meant everything to Izzy. They all knew this, especially Shawn. It wasn't like Vivi wanted Isabelle to go with him, but for him to ask someone else, and for her to find out this way, was devastating. "Am I allowed to kill him yet?" Vivi asked.

"I hate him," Isabelle said as she gasped for air. "I hate him so much!"

As Lane hugged Isabelle, Vivi saw something move from the corner of her eye. Her brother was standing just on the other side of the open doorway to the living room, listening to every word that was said. She shot him a look that could have melted steel and put her arm around Isabelle's shoulder.

"Come on. Let's go downstairs," Vivi said.

"'Kay," Isabelle replied, her voice all watery.

After about ten minutes of incoherence and sobbing, Isabelle finally calmed down. She looked around the wood-paneled basement with heavy-lidded eyes and sniffled.

"What movies did you guys get?" she asked, pulling her hands into the sleeves of her fuzzy sweater.

"We don't have to watch anything if you don't want to," Lane said.

"Yes, we do! She needs the distraction," Vivi put in, reaching for the DVDs.

"True," Isabelle said weakly.

Vivi got up and popped *The Holiday* into the DVD player. Just as the previews were starting up, the door to the basement opened and Vivi saw her brother's dorky brown shoes on the stairs.

"Did we invite you down here?" Vivi shouted.

"I'm just bringing you guys some soda," Marshall replied. He stopped at the bottom of the stairs with a bottle of Mug root beer and three plastic cups. "Seemed like you could maybe use something to drink."

"Thanks, Marshall," Lane said, cutting off the insult Vivi was about to spew.

"I love root beer," Isabelle said blankly.

"Well, there you go." Marshall placed everything on the table and backed up. "I'll be upstairs."

"Again, don't care," Vivi replied.

Marshall shot her an irritated look, but turned around and retreated.

"Vivi, he was just trying to be nice," Isabelle said.

"No. He just has nothing better to do on a Friday night," Vivi said.

She got up, took the stairs two at a time, and latched the old-school lock on the door. On her way back down, she turned off the lights, then settled back on the huge leather sectional between her friends. It was time to put Operation Distract and Empower Izzy into motion. No more diversions.

Vivi tossed a few kernels of popcorn into her mouth as Kate Winslet slammed the door on her idiot ex-boyfriend's face and threw her arms in the air. Vivi couldn't have picked a more perfect post-breakup movie than *The Holiday*. Cameron Diaz and Kate both think their lives are over after breaking up with their respective jerks, and then they both find real happiness. It was an inspired choice, if she did think so herself. She glanced over at Isabelle, half-expecting to see her grinning with romantic inspiration. Isabelle, however, was staring at the floor, chewing on her thumbnail.

"What's the matter?" Vivi said, grabbing the remote to pause the movie. "You're not even watching!"

"I know," Isabelle said. She pulled her knees up and sat back. "I can't stop thinking about Shawn. What do you think he's doing tonight?"

Uh, getting dirty with a certain skank? Vivi thought.

"I don't know, Iz," Lane said.

Isabelle bit her lip. "Do you think we could still get back together?"

Vivi sat up so fast, she dumped half the bowl of popcorn on the cold cement floor. "What?"

"Vivi," Lane said in a warning tone.

"You just told us he asked Tricia to the prom. What are you thinking?" Vivi asked.

"I know," Isabelle said. She ran her hands up into her hair. "I know. It's just . . . I love him so much. Tricia's not going to make him happy. And the prom is still a few weeks away. . . ."

"Omigod, do you even hear yourself?" Vivi blurted, gripping the couch cushions at her sides. "You're worried that *he's* not gonna be happy? You're the one who's miserable!"

"You don't have to attack her," Lane said, zipping her fleece hoodie all the way up as if for protection.

"I was just . . . talking," Isabelle added, averting her gaze.

"You're talking about getting back together with him after he cheated on you. After he asked someone else to the prom," Vivi pointed out. She shoved herself out of her seat and started pacing in front of the TV, where Kate was paused in midcelebration. "I mean, come on. When does it end? Forget all the *little* breakups." She raised her hand to tick off the big ones. "You took him back after he skipped the play last year. You took him back after the sweet sixteen debacle. You took him back after he dumped you on the day of your Stanford interview. Remember how freaked you were? You might not have gotten in because of him! And now he cheats on you and rubs it in your face and you *still* want him? When are you going to see that you deserve much better than Shawn *Slut*tig?"

"Oh, that's very mature," Isabelle sniffed, crossing her arms over her chest.

"Calm down, Viv," Lane said, scooting forward and grabbing a mini quiche off the table.

"Why should I?" Vivi said. "Seriously. It's time for an intervention."

"Don't say something you'll regret," Lane said in her schoolteacher tone. "I mean, if you rip him to shreds and then they get back together—"

"They are not getting back together!" Vivi protested, her hands on her hips.

"Uh, I'm right here." Isabelle raised her hand, sounding frustrated. "And you can't tell me what to do, Viv."

"Well, I should be able to," Vivi replied, her blood boiling. "Clearly you're incapable of making your own decisions. I want you to be happy, and all Shawn does is make you miserable. Your relationship with him is all one-sided."

Isabelle's face screwed up in consternation, and she stood, facing off with Vivi over the coffee table. "Oh, please. What do you know about relationships? You haven't had one that's lasted more than a month since Daniel! Shawn and I have been together for four years!"

"Probably more like two if you factor in all the times you've broken up," Vivi shot back.

"You guys—," Lane said.

"Well, at least I'm not always reeling guys in and then torturing them until they dump me!" Isabelle replied.

Vivi felt as if she'd been slapped. "What?"

"Oh God, Viv. I'm sorry," Isabelle said. She briefly covered her mouth with her hand. "I didn't mean that."

Vivi had to sit down again. Was that really what her friends thought she did? Systematically tortured guys?

"I'm sorry, Vivi," Isabelle repeated. "Really."

Lane looked at Vivi hopefully. Vivi took a deep breath and combed her fingers through her thick ponytail. She was a champion at the uncalled-for word bomb. There was no way she could hold it against Isabelle without being a huge hypocrite. Especially in Izzy's current state.

"It's okay," Vivi said, grabbing Izzy's hand and squeezing it.

Isabelle took a deep breath and turned to fold up the afghan she'd been huddled under all night long. "I should just go."

"What? We haven't even gotten to the ice cream yet," Lane protested.

"I'm really not in the mood for ice cream," Isabelle said apologetically.

Vivi suddenly felt desperate. This whole night had been intended to distract Isabelle and help her get over Shawn, and it hadn't worked in the slightest.

"Don't go, Iz," Vivi said. "I'm sorry. I didn't mean to attack you. I just . . . I don't want you to go backward. I mean, you're gonna be at Stanford next year. It's gonna be a whole new world, you know? New people, new *guys*. . . . Why would you want to go backward?"

Isabelle's eyes watered as she shrugged. "I love him. I'm sorry I can't just turn that off."

She took a step past Vivi and grabbed her pink Nine West raincoat and Kate Spade overnight bag off the floor. "Thanks for trying, guys. I do appreciate it. I just kind of want my own bed right now, you know?"

Vivi and Lane exchanged a defeated look. "We know."

They walked Isabelle upstairs, and Vivi gave her a hug before sending her off to her car. When Vivi closed the door, her shoulders sagged.

"How are we ever going to get her over him if she doesn't want to?" she asked.

Lane shook her head. "I don't know."

Vivi stared at the tiled floor of the foyer. "You know, I could have a long relationship if I wanted one. It's just that the guys at school can't handle me."

"I know."

Lane put her arm around Vivi's back and Vivi rested the side of her head atop Lane's. Together they shuffled toward the kitchen with its 1970s avocado countertops and yellow Formica table. Vivi's mother loved kitch, and therefore hadn't changed one thing in their kitchen since buying the house from an elderly couple when Vivi was still in kindergarten. Vivi yanked open the ancient freezer and took out a few pints of ice cream while Lane went for spoons and bowls and toppings. Within two minutes they had put together a pair of towering sundaes. Vivi took a huge bite, dripping chocolate sauce down over her hand. She grabbed a napkin from the ceramic cow holder at the center of the kitchen table and sighed.

"All right. That's it," she said, sitting up straight.

"What's it?" Lane asked warily, nearly losing some of her ice cream out the side of her mouth.

"We are going to come up with a way to keep Isabelle away from Sluttig," Vivi said, determined.

"Like what? Kidnapping?" Lane asked.

Vivi narrowed her eyes, imagining Shawn tied up in a rat-infested basement somewhere, wearing nothing but dirty rags and begging for mercy. "Nothing that drastic," she said. She grabbed her bowl and spoon and a few more napkins. "Come on. Let's go up to my room and brainstorm."

"But what about the movie?" Lane asked, stalling.

"Screw the movie," Vivi said, shoving another huge wad of ice cream into her mouth. "This is much more important. We have to save Izzy."

✳ ✳ ✳

"Maybe we could find her a therapist, you know?" Vivi babbled, pacing back and forth behind Lane, who was sitting at the computer in Vivi's bedroom. She had to step over the piles of clothes, books, and random crap all over the floor, and she kept kicking stuff out of her way. "Or a hypnotist! Someone who could deprogram her. Google that!"

"Yeah, sure. I'm on it," Lane lied, typing her password into the MySpace login page.

"Not that she'd go, because apparently she doesn't see this

whole thing as a problem, which is totally OOC," Vivi said, looking at the ceiling.

Lane smirked. "You sound like Curtis."

"Oh, crap! I do," Vivi said, holding her head. "Your little love bug has totally infiltrated my brain," she teased.

"He is not my love bug," Lane said, pulling her ponytail over her shoulder to toy with it.

"Whatever you say," Vivi replied, sitting down on the edge of her unmade bed. She crossed her legs and bounced the top leg around as if she were stirring something. "I don't know why you don't just ask him to the prom already. I mean, you're just as bad as Isabelle except you can't get up the guts to *get* the guy and she can't get up the guts to *lose* the guy. Why won't you just ask him to the prom? What's the worst that could happen?"

"Umm . . . he could run screaming in the other direction and never speak to me again, which would break up our entire group and change our lives forever," Lane recited automatically.

"Oh. Yeah. That would suck," Vivi replied, looking irritated that Lane actually made some sense. "Whatever—back to Isabelle. What are we going to do?"

"I don't know," Lane said lightly. She knew better than to encourage Vivi. If she did, this rant might sooner or later become an actual plan, and Lane knew from experience that Vivi's plans rarely worked out for the best. But sometimes, if she was lucky, Vivi would just babble with no direction until she tired herself out and the whole thing would come to nothing.

Lane had already navigated to her in-box and was psyched to see a message from SurfBoy07 at the top of the list. He was supposed to be critiquing her last painting. SurfBoy07 was an art student from California whom she'd met months ago on the site. After a few IM conversations, they had realized they both harbored a love of art and a need for unbiased feedback from someone outside their regular classes. They had started sending jpegs of their work back and forth. and Lane felt that her painting had much improved, thanks to his comments. She crossed her fingers for luck and clicked his message.

"Oh! Maybe we could find a way to make Shawn totally unappealing to her," Vivi continued, pushing herself off her bed to start pacing again. "I mean, the guy *is* hot—I'll give him that. Maybe that's how Izzy sees past all the other crap, right? Maybe we should break into his house and shave his head!"

"I draw the line at breaking and entering," Lane said as she read through SurfBoy07's message.

> Hey Penny Lane,
> This painting is amazing. Your use of shading and shadow has improved dramatically. Really. Your best work yet. Would it be lame to admit I'm jealous?
> ☺
> SB07

Lane's heart expanded, and she could barely contain a grin. This was exactly the message she'd been hoping for. Her best work yet. SurfBoy07 was in a real art program at a great school. If he loved it, then it would have to earn an A.

"Whoa. Who's that?" Vivi stopped and stared over Lane's shoulder. Lane glanced at SurfBoy07's picture. With his sun-kissed good looks and friendly smile, he *was* rather Oakley-icious.

"He's just a MySpace friend of mine," Lane said, trying to contain her critique-related glee so that Vivi wouldn't grill her about it. "He's an artist. We chat sometimes."

"Omigod. There's no way that's his real picture," Vivi said. She reached around Lane's back and grabbed the mouse, scrolling quickly down SurfBoy's page. "He totally stole that off the Hollister website or something."

"No, he didn't. I asked about the picture. That's totally him," Lane protested.

"No way." Vivi stood up straight. "No real guy is that hot."

"Do you have any idea how insane you sound? Some-body *is* that hot because that picture is of somebody," Lane told her.

"Well, it's not SurfBoy07. No one that gorgeous has time to be on MySpace," Vivi said. "Sorry to tell you this, Lane, but he has to be a fake."

Vivi scoffed, like Lane was ridiculous, and paced away. Lane's heart hurt. Why did Vivi have to tear her down like that? Couldn't Lane ever be right about anything?

"Wait a minute! That's it!" Vivi announced suddenly.

All the tiny hairs on the back of Lane's neck stood on end. "What? What's it?"

"A fake!" Vivi whirled around, her eyes bright. She grabbed the arms of the chair and twirled Lane toward her. "We'll make up a guy for Isabelle on MySpace! Someone who will totally take her mind off that skeezoid Sluttig."

Lane's skin tightened as her entire body filled with dread. Crap. Crappity crap crap. "What?"

"Come on! Who knows Isabelle better than we do? We can make up her perfect guy," Vivi said, clasping her hands together. "We can make him a little bit dangerous, you know, because we know she likes that. But we can also give him a life! Make him interesting! Shawn's only interests are smoking, playing three chords on his guitar, and being a jackass. We can do *so* much better than that. And MySpace is the perfect place to do it. We can make him as incredible as we want him to be!"

Lane squirmed in the chair. "Please tell me you're kidding."

"Do I look like I'm kidding?" Vivi asked, putting her hands in the front pocket of her hoodie.

Lane stared into her friend's excited green eyes. "Unfortunately, no."

"Good," Vivi said with a grin. "Now get out of my chair."

★ ★ ★ *three* ★ ★ ★

"Unbelievable," Vivi said, leaning back in her chair and crooking her arms behind her neck. She checked her Nike sports watch. "Less than an hour to make up a whole person."

"You sure you don't want to give him a cool screen name?" Lane asked from the rickety old kitchen chair next to Vivi. "Most people have them."

"That's all right, *Penny Lane*," Vivi said facetiously. "Brandon is too cool for that."

Lane rolled her eyes at the dig.

"What? Come on. You're the one who said he should be a man of few words—which was totally perfect, by the way," Vivi said, trying to appease Lane with a compliment. She reached for the mouse and scrolled up. "Would a guy whose 'About me' reads only, 'Drums. Summer. Books. Coffee—black,' really make up a doofy name for himself?"

Lane considered this with a thoughtful frown. "Okay. Good point."

They both leaned back again to admire their work. The cool black-and-brown background had been cribbed from one of Lane's other male friends—she seemed to have a lot, which surprised Vivi—but then maybe her friend was better at talking to guys online than in person. Lane had also constructed some killer favorites lists. They were spare, but they included a few of Isabelle's faves, and had been rounded out by choices that were convincingly guy stuff like *The Art of War, Junk Brothers,* and select Adam Sandler movies.

Then, the pièce de résistance: his profile picture. A photo of a black-and-white boxer dog they had lifted from some other guy's page. Isabelle loved dogs. Brandon having his pup as his picture might even distract Izzy from the fact that she didn't actually know what the guy looked like. They'd even put "My dog Henley" in his "Heroes" section. Vivi's most inspired idea of the night.

"It's perfect," Vivi said, satisfied.

"Not quite," Lane told her, reaching for the mouse. "He needs some friends."

"What do you mean?" Vivi asked.

"We can't just have him add Isabelle first. He'll look like a loser stalker," Lane pointed out. She navigated to her own page and went to her friend space. "Here. We'll find some people that are online right now and send them friend requests."

"Lane, I think you might be good at this deception thing," Vivi said, impressed.

"I won't let it go to my head," Lane replied with a touch

of sarcasm. She hadn't let Vivi forget for one moment that she disapproved of this whole plan, but she blushed slightly anyway.

Within fifteen minutes, Brandon had eleven new friends and two comments about how cool his dog was.

"I can't believe how many people have nothing better to do on a Friday night than this," Vivi said, shaking her head.

"Including us," Lane replied.

"Yes, but we're on a mission," Vivi pointed out. She dropped forward and put her feet on the ground, pulling the keyboard to her. "Okay. Let's do this."

"Now? You're gonna message her now?" Lane was panicked.

"Why wait?" Vivi asked.

"Let's just think about this a sec," Lane said, getting up. "I mean, yeah, creating Mr. Perfect has been fun, but do we want to mess with her like this?"

"We're not messing with her," Vivi protested. "We're helping her see the light at the end of the tunnel. She needs to know there are other options out there."

"Yeah, but—"

"Lane. It's totally harmless," Vivi told her, tilting her head. "I mean, any real guy could add her on here at any second and serve the exact same purpose. We just can't wait that long. Don't be a wuss."

Lane took a deep breath, and Vivi knew she had her. Her eyes trailed to the computer screen, open to Isabelle's pretty white-and-pink page. The photo of Isabelle from Lane's bowling birthday party last February grinned back at them.

Lane squeezed her eyes closed. "All right, fine. Let's get this over with."

"Yes! What should I write?" Vivi asked, her fingers hovering over the keyboard. She started to type. "Hey. You're hot. Where do you—?"

"Vivi!" Lane blurted.

"What?"

"You're hot? You've gotta be kidding me," Lane said.

"What? I'm trying to sound like a guy," Vivi replied, eyes wide. She turned her hands palm up over the keyboard. "Think you can do better?"

Lane shrugged. "Maybe . . ."

"Fine," Vivi said, standing up in a huff. "Go ahead."

Lane cleared her throat. Tentatively, she stepped up to the keyboard. Vivi stood and looked over her shoulder while she typed.

> Hey,
> Your dog looks exactly like my uncle Franklin. It's very weird.
> Does he smell like coffee and cigarettes, too?
> —Brandon

For a long moment, Vivi stared at the message, completely baffled. "His uncle Franklin? What are you—?" Then, it hit her, and she started to think that Lane really might be an evil genius. "Oh! Because she always says she thinks Buster is part dog, part old man!"

"Exactly," Lane said, crossing her arms over her chest.

"It's perfect." Vivi reached over and hit SEND.

"Wait!" Lane blurted.

"Too late," Vivi said, slapping her hands together. She navigated back to Brandon's page and preened. "Operation Skewer Sluttig is now in motion."

"But I didn't read it over!" Lane cried.

"So? I did. It was perfect," Vivi replied.

"What if she writes back?" Lane asked.

Vivi put her hands on Lane's bony shoulders and looked her in the eye. "Dial down the drama, okay? It's fine."

Lane took a deep breath and nodded shakily. "Okay."

"Besides, look at her page. She's not even online." Vivi released Lane and grabbed a towel off her floor, heading for the bathroom. "She said she was going to bed when she got home. She probably won't even get it until the morning."

"Right. Right," Lane said, crouching down next to her bag and unzipping it. "She's gotta be sleeping by now." She yanked her blue Paul Frank toiletries bag out and stood, but after one glance at the computer, she completely froze. "Uh. Vivi?"

"Yeah?"

"She wrote back," Lane said.

Vivi's heart stopped for a full five seconds. "Already? But she's not—"

"You can cover up the fact that you're online," Lane said, her voice growing shrill. "Something we probably should have done since right now she can tell that we—that Brandon—is on."

Vivi's eyes widened, and she walked over to the desk. "Wait, so she's waiting for us to reply?"

"Maybe! I mean, she knows we're . . . he's . . . oh God!" Lane cried, collapsing onto the end of Vivi's bed. She clutched her toiletries bag with both hands, shaking up the contents like a rattle. "I thought she was going to bed!"

"Well, that was a big lie," Vivi said, putting her hands on her hips.

"What're we gonna do? What're we gonna do?" Lane asked. She dropped the bag as if the monkeys all over it had come to life and bitten her fingers. She shook her hands in front of her as her face grew beet red.

"Calm down," Vivi said, rolling her eyes. "Let's just read the message and see what she says."

She sat down at the computer and opened Isabelle's message.

> OMG! That is TOO funny. I've always thought that Buster had an old man trapped inside of him. Nice to know someone else sees it, too. New to MySpace, huh? Welcome. Hope you'll accept my friend request. So what are you doing home on a Friday night? WB!
> Izzy

"She totally loves him," Vivi said, feeling giddy.

"She totally knows we're here!" Lane said through her teeth, pressing her hands into the back of Vivi's chair. "I mean, *he's* here!"

Suddenly an IM popped up on the screen, and Lane screamed, grabbing Vivi like some psycho killer had just broken in.

> **IzzyBelly:** I'm not a stalker. Just bored. Are you there?

"Oh my God. Oh my God. What do we say?" Lane cried,

pressing down hard on the back of Vivi's chair.

Vivi's blood rushed in her ears, and everything felt suddenly shaky. "Will you calm down? You're freaking me out!"

"Well, what's she doing? This isn't like her!"

"Maybe she's taking our advice. Trying to move on?" Vivi said hopefully, pushing back her sweatshirt sleeves.

"We have to write back," Lane told her. "She's waiting. If we don't write back, she's gonna feel rejected all over again."

"Okay." Vivi put her fingers on the keyboard. They were trembling. Lane's psychotic tension was rubbing off on her. If she screwed up, this plan would be over before it ever got off the ground. But if she said the *right* thing—whatever it was Isabelle needed to hear—everything could change for the better. "What do I say?"

"What would a *guy* say?" Lane asked, her hands clasped.

"I don't know," Vivi replied. "Contrary to some people's asinine jokes, I'm not one."

The clock at the bottom right corner of her screen clicked over from 11:31 to 11:32. Vivi's heart rate ratcheted up a notch. On the other side of town, Isabelle was staring at her computer screen, waiting for the perfect response.

"I can't take it!" Vivi blurted, backing away from the computer. "This is too intense!"

"Vivi! We have to do something!" Lane turned around in a circle like a dog looking for a spot to lie down, wringing her hands the whole way. Down the hall, Death Cab for Cutie blared out from tinny speakers. Lane suddenly stopped, facing the door. "Marshall!" she announced.

"What?" Vivi demanded.

"Marshall's a guy!" Lane flew out of the room and down the hallway.

"That's debatable!" Vivi called, following her to the hall.

Lane walked right through the open door to Marshall's room and came back two seconds later, steering a pajama-clad Marshall toward Vivi by his shoulders.

"This is never gonna work," Vivi said, raising her hands—even though she had no alternative in mind.

"Um, what's never gonna work?" Marshall asked warily.

Lane stopped him next to the desk and pulled out the chair. "Sit," she ordered.

"Why?" Marshall was understandably concerned.

"Lane. Marshall has more estrogen in his veins than I do," Vivi said.

"Estrogen isn't in your veins," Marshall corrected, rolling his eyes. "And I do not."

"And see? He's a complete brain! He's not Brandon," Vivi said.

"Brandon *is* a brain," Lane replied. "Smart guys are sexy."

"They are?" Marshall asked, brightening slightly.

"Not this one," Vivi muttered.

"Marshall, please just sit?" Lane begged.

Marshall did as he was asked, though he still looked concerned. He kept his butt near the edge of the chair as if ready to bolt at any second. Like he could really make it out the door if Vivi wanted to stop him.

"We don't need him," Vivi said.

"Yes, we do. We need a guy to talk to her. We are not guys.

Marshall, however, is," Lane explained calmly and logically, her hands on her hips.

Vivi opened her mouth, but Marshall reached up and slapped his hand over it. "Don't say whatever you're thinking of saying."

Vivi rolled her eyes and turned away—her method of consenting to involving Marshall, however ill-fated the idea was.

Lane pressed her hands into the arms of the chair and looked Marshall in the eye. "Okay, here's the deal. We just made up a fake guy for Isabelle on MySpace and now she's IMing him. You have to talk to her for us," Lane said.

What little color there was in Marshall's face drained out of it. He glanced at the computer screen in fear, as if it were scrolling satanic messages. "Wait, if I type back, I'm typing to Isabelle?"

"Yes! And she's waiting," Vivi said, leaning in close to Marshall's face for emphasis.

"Are you guys out of your minds?" Marshall asked, scooting back and looking back and forth between them.

"I think that's obvious, don't you?" Lane said. "Now please! Type!"

"Well . . . I . . . who is this guy?" Marshall asked, sinking down into the chair slightly.

"He's a drummer. Very cool. Kind of monosyllabic and, you know, hot," Lane said.

"So your complete opposite," Vivi put in, cocking her head to the side.

"Vivi!" Lane said through her teeth. "But he's also smart,

and well read. Just like you." Lane told him. "Please, Marshall? Pretty please?"

Behind her, Vivi scoffed. She couldn't believe she was letting this happen. But she knew that if she tried to IM with Isabelle, she would say something personal that would give her away, and she couldn't let that happen. Marshall was as good a choice as any. He'd barely ever said a word to Isabelle, anyway, so there was no way he could reveal himself.

"Fine," Marshall said finally, though he looked ready to hurl. "Monosyllabic, huh?"

"Yes!" Lane said.

Marshall cleared his throat and wiped his palms on his black sweatpants. He typed and hit SEND.

Brandon: I'm here.

"Well, I could have come up with that!" Vivi chided.

"Shhhh!" Lane said.

IzzyBelly: Nothing to do in Connecticut on Fridays?

"Connecticut?" Marshall asked, looking at Lane for guidance.

"That's where he's from," Lane replied.

She sat down on the extra chair and pulled it closer to the desk. Vivi picked up her purple beanbag chair and dropped it next to Marshall, settling in on his other side. Marshall's fingers trembled as they hovered over the keys.

Brandon: Probably about as much as there is to do in Jersey.

IzzyBelly: Touche. ☺

Vivi laughed and clapped her hands together. "She likes it!"

Both Marshall and Lane visibly relaxed.

"Still think this was a bad idea?" Vivi asked Lane, peeking around Marshall.

"We'll see," Lane said, trying to stifle a smile.

"Oh, please. Operation Skewer Sluttig is in full effect, and it was all me," Vivi said with a sniff, crossing her arms over her chest. "Geniuses are never appreciated in their own time."

★ ★ ★ *four* ★ ★ ★

Lane pressed her lips together and checked out her gloss in her locker mirror, then smoothed the front of her new floaty, baby blue blouse from Anthropologie. Normally she wouldn't wear something so special to school, but today, she had a date with Curtis. Well, not a date, exactly. They were studying for their Calc exam the next day. But they were going to walk home from school together and hang out until dinner, which was a nice chunk of one-on-one Curtis in one day. Her heart went all fluttery just thinking about it, and she had no idea how she was supposed to get through eight whole class periods. She felt like she might not actually be able to wait. Like she might spontaneously combust in the process.

"Lane!"

She flinched, feeling as if she'd been caught at something, then realized all she'd been doing was standing at her locker. Vivi barreled toward her, all bright eyes and smiles, paying no attention to the pack of freshmen who had to dodge out of her way to avoid being trampled. She was wearing her jeans and a fitted blue American Eagle hoodie, and her hair was smoothed back in a headband and brushed to a gloss. This was a good-mood outfit for Vivi. She never spent more than five minutes in front of a mirror unless she was in a very happy place.

"Hey! So, did you talk to Isabelle yet?" Vivi asked, leaning against the locker next to Lane's.

Lane smiled slightly. When Vivi was in the midst of a plan, it was pretty much all she talked about. All she thought about. Basically, the plan became her life.

"I talked to her last night," Lane told her blithely. Because she knew that being blithe and vague would drive Vivi crazy.

"Well? How did she sound? Did she mention Brandon?" Vivi whispered, glancing over her shoulder.

"Nope," Lane said, slowly taking her books out of her upper locker.

"No? Come on. You've got to be kidding. She and Marshall IM'd all freaking weekend. I barely left my room, keeping an eye on him," Vivi said, turning around to kick her heel back against the lockers. "She's never going to get over that jackass, is she?"

Lane decided to take pity on her friend. "I haven't told you the good news yet, Viv."

Vivi's eyebrows shot up, and she turned and huddled toward Lane. "Good news? What good news?"

Lane leaned in, savoring the moment. "She didn't talk about Shawn either. Not one single word. No 'Will we get back together?' No 'Why hasn't he called me?' No 'Do you think he's with Tricia right now?' Nothing. And we were on the phone for at least an hour."

The news had its desired affect. Vivi's entire face lit up. "Not one word?"

"Not one word."

Vivi laid her hand out to be slapped, and Lane slid her palm across it with a smirk. At first she had thought that Vivi's MySpace plan was ridiculous and fraught with potential disaster. But Isabelle had sounded good on the phone last night. Almost happy. And after more than a week of self-doubt and misery, hearing her friend laugh was enough to get Lane behind the Brandon plan. At least for now.

"Hey, girls!"

Lane and Vivi looked up to find Isabelle striding toward them. Her hair was neatly brushed, her makeup was in place, and she was wearing her favorite red top and cute floral skirt. Lane went giddy at the very sight of her.

"She's ba-ack," Vivi sang under her breath.

"She *so* is," Lane agreed.

"Come on," Isabelle said as she passed them by. "I need a bathroom run before homeroom."

Lane happily slammed her locker shut, and she and Vivi flanked Isabelle on their way down the hallway. They were almost to the bathroom door when Shawn Littig himself came around the corner, looking as bad-boy hot as ever, all unshaven and messy hair, wearing a beat-up long-sleeved thermal T-shirt. Lane's heart caught with nervousness at the sight of him, so she could only imagine what Isabelle's heart was doing. Vivi cursed under her breath.

"Hey, Belle," Shawn said, leaning against the wall and giving her his puppy dog eyes. This was how he always sucked Isabelle in. Playing the bad boy who was bad only because he was all tortured and needy.

This is it. This is where the whole plan goes to crap, Lane thought.

But Isabelle didn't stop. She simply breezed right by him, shoved open the bathroom door, and disappeared. Lane paused for a second, completely stunned, and glanced at Shawn over her shoulder. He looked as baffled as she was.

"That, my friend, is the Brandon Effect," Vivi said quietly.

"Impressive," Lane said.

"I know," Vivi said. "Maybe you'll start listening to my Curtis advice now."

Lane rolled her eyes as Vivi walked into the bathroom, but she was starting to wonder. Maybe Vivi *was* right about the Curtis situation. Maybe . . . it was time to start listening to her best friend.

✳ ✳ ✳

Lane walked toward the bleachers after school, her heart pounding against her rib cage, trying to get out. All day she'd been thinking about Vivi and Isabelle and Shawn and Brandon. All day she'd been psyching herself up to do the deed. To follow Vivi's advice. To open her mouth and just say it:

"Wanna go to the prom with me?" About five minutes earlier, she'd been ready. She'd been absolutely, positively sure that she could do it. But now, seeing Curtis up ahead chatting with some of the guys, she knew the exact opposite was true.

There was no way she could do this. No way in hell.

But at least then you'll know, she told herself. *At least then you can stop feeling so nauseated all the time.*

Curtis spotted her and grinned, lifting a hand in greeting. Lane's heart soared.

"Just do it," she said under her breath. "You can do it."

"Hey, Lane!" Curtis said when she finally got close enough.

"Hey," she replied, smoothing a piece of her hair over her shoulder.

She was out of breath, and not from the walk. Behind him, a few of his friends bounced a basketball around on the outdoor court.

"You ready to go?" she asked, consciously trying not to jump up and down.

Curtis pressed his teeth together and cocked his head to the side. His floppy hair fell adorably across his eyes, and he smoothed it out of the way. "Actually, I can't."

Lane went hot with disappointment. "What do you mean?"

"I totally forgot I promised the guys I'd play three on three today," Curtis said, gesturing over his shoulder. "If I don't stay, they've got uneven teams."

"But what about the exam?" Lane said, feeling lame even as she said it.

"We still have tomorrow to study," he said. "I can cram."

Lane felt tears prickling behind her eyes, which made her feel like a total loser. And that just made her want to cry more. She'd been looking forward to this all day long. It was all she'd thought about. But clearly, Curtis didn't care about being with her one bit.

"Oh. Okay," she said finally, putting her hair behind her ears.

"Listen, I have a kind of huge favor to ask," he said.

"What's up?" Lane asked. Maybe the favor at least involved spending some time with him at some point this week.

"Can you ride my bike home for me?" Curtis asked, biting his lip winsomely. "Jeff's gonna drive me home later, and he just has his Mustang."

Lane glanced at his mountain bike, which was lying in the dirt nearby. Getting it home wouldn't be a major deal, considering they lived right next door to each other, but it wasn't exactly romantic.

"Lane?" Curtis prompted, bending a little to look her in the eyes.

"Oh, uh, sure," she said.

"I mean, unless you want to stick around and watch," Curtis suggested, grinning. "I could always use another cheerleader."

For a split second, Lane considered it. If he wanted her to stay, maybe she should. But then she looked over his shoulder and saw that Kim Wolfe and a few other girls from her class were already kicked back in the bleachers, chatting on cell phones and half-watching the guys. It wasn't like it was a special invitation. Apparently, lots of girls were involved.

"Nah. That's okay," Lane said. "I should probably just go home and study."

"You're gonna make me feel guilty," Curtis joked. He knocked her shoulder with his fist, and she smiled. Even when she was upset, he could so easily make her smile. "So you'll take the bike?"

"Yeah. Have fun," Lane said.

"Thanks! I'll call ya later, okay?"

"Yep."

Curtis turned and jogged toward the court, where the girls in the stands greeted him with hoots and hollers. Lane crouched down and lifted Curtis's bike out of the dirt. As she stood up, the handlebar dragged across the front of her blouse, leaving a big brown smear.

"Perfect," Lane said under her breath as cheers erupted behind her. "Just perfect."

★ ★ ★   *five*   ★ ★ ★

Vivi walked into her room after track practice to find her brother already sitting at her computer.

"God! You scared the crap outta me," she said, throwing her bags down on the floor.

"Sorry. History paper," Marshall replied without looking up. Of course. That was her brother. He hadn't even changed after school—he was still wearing the ridiculously preppy polo shirt and khakis he'd worn that day. He'd probably come through the door, had a healthy snack of apples and water, and come right upstairs to work. How they were from the same gene pool, Vivi had no idea.

"I can't wait until I get my new computer." Vivi threw her duffel bag onto her unmade bed and sat down to peel off her sneakers. "Then you can have this one and leave me alone."

Marshall tipped his head back in frustration, and his blond bangs fell back from his forehead.

"Hey! Your hair isn't gelled into a helmet today," Vivi noticed. "What gives?"

Marshall's face grew blotchy, and it was clearly taking an effort for him to keep from looking at her. "Just . . . trying something new."

Vivi stood up and leaned back against her desk next to him to check it out. "It looks nice."

His blotchiness deepened. "Thanks."

"So, is Isabelle online?" Vivi asked, gesturing at the screen.

"How would I know?" Marshall replied.

"Uhh . . . because you've got the MySpace window minimized right there," Vivi replied. "Why don't you check?"

Marshall blinked. "Oh, yeah. I forgot that was there."

He clicked on the bar, and the MySpace screen popped up. Brandon's MySpace screen, to be exact.

"What were you doing on Brandon's MySpace page?" she asked. "And how did you get the password?"

"First of all, your password has been 'double-v' since the beginning of time," Marshall said. "And second, I wasn't doing anything. I was just checking it out. Seeing what you and Lane think a guy's page should be like. I didn't really get much of a chance over the weekend with you ordering me around and breathing down my neck."

"Oh," Vivi said. She pulled her second chair over, turned it around, and straddled. "So? How'd we do?" she asked, resting her arms on the back of the chair.

"Actually, he seems pretty cool," Marshall conceded, clicking on VIEW: MY PROFILE.

"Good," Vivi replied. She noticed that the ONLINE NOW

icon was flashing next to Isabelle's name on Brandon's top friends. A rush of excitement shot through her. "Look! She's on. Let's IM her."

"Right now?" Marshall said, looking at Lane with wide eyes.

"No. Next Wednesday," Vivi said, rolling her eyes. "Just ask her what she's up to."

Marshall took a deep breath and cleared his throat. "Fine. But only for a few minutes. I have to get back to my paper."

"I promise I will get you back to your precious homework before you know it."

He ignored her and opened the IM window.

> **Brandon:** Hey. What's up?
> **IzzyBelly:** Hi! Not much. How are you?
> **Brandon:** Fine. What're you doing?
> **IzzyBelly:** Stressing actually.

Vivi and Marshall exchanged a glance. "About what?" Vivi asked.

Marshall typed.

> **Brandon:** About what?
> **IzzyBelly:** Prom. Everyone's talking about it and I don't have a date. Too bad you live so far . . . LOL I don't know. It just feels like there's no one to go with.

"This is perfect!" Vivi said, getting up and turning the chair around so she could lean toward the screen. "Tell her you're sure she's going to find a date. Tell her she's so amazing there are probably hundreds of guys who want to go with her."

Brandon: Please. I bet a lot of guys would kill to go with you.

"Nice edit," Vivi said, impressed, leaning her elbow on the desk.

Marshall blushed and shrugged.

IzzyBelly: I wish. There's no one good in my class. At least no one that doesn't have a date already.

Vivi opened her mouth to make a suggestion, but Marshall was already typing.

Brandon: What about other classes? Juniors, maybe?

He hit SEND before Vivi could stop him, so instead, she whacked him across the back of his blond head.

"Hey! Ow!" Marshall protested, rubbing the spot Vivi hit.

"Don't send her stuff without my approval!" Vivi said.

"Why not? You liked the last thing I wrote!" Marshall pointed out.

Vivi pressed her lips together. "All right, fine. But at least let me read it first."

Marshall huffed a sigh. "Whatever."

They both stared at the screen. It was taking Isabelle a while to type back.

"Where'd she go?" Vivi demanded. "Dammit, Marshall. You scared her away! Why the hell did you have to mention the juniors? Your class is like a walking horror movie. She probably thinks you're an idiot now."

"I'm sorry, I just—"

Suddenly another message popped up. Vivi and Marshall fell silent.

> **IzzyBelly:** Maybe. I don't know. It's just . . . my ex has been texting me all day today. Just got another one from him. I think he might want to get back together. And I always imagined we'd go to the prom. . . .

"Oh, no! No, no, no!" Vivi jumped up and dug through her cluttered bag for her cell phone. When she finally unearthed it, she hit speed-dial three for Isabelle and clutched the phone to her ear. She was going to save this girl from herself if it killed her.

"What're you doing?" Marshall gasped, now standing as well.

"I'm calling her," Vivi replied, pacing in front of her bed. "She can't be talking to Sluttig. There's no way."

"But you're not supposed to *know* that!" Marshall pointed out.

Vivi's heart dropped just as Isabelle picked up the phone. She stared at Marshall, eyes wide, like she'd just been called on in class and had no idea what the question was. What was she going to say? What the hell was she *thinking*?

"Hey, Vivi," Isabelle said. "What's up?"

"Uh, nothing," Vivi replied, heart pounding. "What's up with you?"

There was a pause. "Nothing . . . You called me."

"Oh, right. I did, didn't I?" Vivi improvised. Marshall tipped his head back and covered his face with his hands. "Uh . . . whatcha doing?"

"Not much," Isabelle replied. In the background, Vivi could hear Isabelle typing. Two seconds later, another IM popped up on her computer screen. She and Marshall both stared at it like it was about to explode.

IzzyBelly: Still there?

Vivi waved at Marshall to sit down and type back. Marshall looked like he was in the midst of an extremely premature heart attack, but he did as he was told. He typed something quickly, and the keyboard sounded like a jackhammer. Cursing to herself, Vivi got on her bed and curled into the far corner of the room.

"Not much, huh?" she said loudly, trying to cover the sound of typing. "Sounds like you're on the computer. Are you IMing someone?"

Instantly Marshall stopped typing and shot her an exasperated look. On the other end of the line, Isabelle was silent. Vivi closed her eyes and held her breath. What was she thinking?

"Actually . . . yeah," Isabelle said finally. "And I kind of have to go. Unless . . . was there something you wanted to talk about?"

"No. Not really," Vivi replied. "I'll talk to you later, okay? Bye!"

She turned off the phone without waiting for a reply and collapsed back on her bed, where a pillow promptly hit her in the face.

"Hey!" she shouted, sitting up and throwing the pillow back at Marshall.

"So much for you being a genius!" Marshall blurted, catching the pillow easily. "You almost gave us away! She could have been e-mailing someone or working on a paper. What're you supposed to be, psychic now?"

"God. Chill out, Marshall. She doesn't suspect anything," Vivi said grouchily, lying down on her side, facing Marshall. "Besides, this was my idea. I can give it away if I want to."

"Well? What did she say about Shawn?" Marshall asked. He put the pillow down and crossed his arms over his chest. His biceps bulged slightly. Apparently he had been working out behind her back. Weird. "Are they getting back together?"

"She didn't say anything. Brandon probably has a better chance of finding out the truth than I do," she said, glaring at the computer. "She knows I hate the guy."

"That's great, Viv. It's nice to know you've alienated your friends so much, they won't even talk to you about life-altering decisions," Marshall said, swiveling from left to right in the desk chair.

"What do you know about having friends?" Vivi shot back.

Marshall's jaw dropped slightly. "I have friends!"

"The people you work with at Barnes and Noble don't count," Vivi replied.

"You suck, Viv, you know that?" Marshall said. He got up, grabbed his books, and closed the MySpace screen. "I'll finish my paper later."

"See ya!" Vivi said, following him to the door so she could slam it.

Alone in her room, she realized that on some level, Marshall was right. She couldn't help if Izzy refused to talk to her about Shawn *or* Brandon. Tomorrow she was going to have to get the girl to open up, and she was going to have to talk her out of getting back together with Shawn, once and for all.

＊ ＊ ＊

"I think I might ask Shawn to the prom," Isabelle announced, standing in the center of her pink-and-white Laura Ashley bedroom.

"What? No!" Vivi cried, sitting up straight on the floral window seat.

"I thought he was going with Tricia," Lane offered. She put the basketball trophy she was toying with back on the jam-packed award shelf on the wall.

"I think she lied. He said they've talked about it, but he hasn't actually asked her," Isabelle said, making a face.

"So you guys are talking again," Vivi said flatly. She turned sideways, bringing her feet up on the pristine cushion. "Great."

"Just e-mailing and texting . . . mostly," Isabelle replied, walking over to knock Vivi's feet down again, which Vivi had been fully expecting. "We're working our way up to actual talking."

"I'm working my way up to not vomiting," Vivi said, glaring up at her friend.

"That's nice. Very supportive," Isabelle shot back.

Frustrated, Vivi put her head in her hands and looked over at Lane, who sat on the canopied bed with her tongue tied, as usual. If Isabelle went to the prom with Shawn, she would be completely sucked back in, and they would spend the entire summer breaking up and getting back together. For all Vivi knew, Shawn could convince Isabelle not to go away to school next year because it would destroy their star-crossed love. He had that kind of power over her.

Isabelle paced over to her big wooden desk and leaned back against it, twisting her silver ring around and around her finger.

"I know you guys don't like Shawn. Obviously," she began. "But I can't help how I feel. Besides, you don't know him like I do."

Vivi had to grip the cushion under her butt to keep from rolling her eyes. How many times had she heard this exact speech?

"His parents are, like, evil. Like *Oliver Twist* evil. They're so mean to him, you have no idea. I'm all he's got, you know? I'm the only person in the world who really cares about him," Isabelle rambled, still twisting her ring around her finger. "I don't know . . . maybe this thing with Tricia is just, like, separation anxiety because I'm going away next year."

"You're gonna use your psych class to make excuses for him?" Vivi blurted.

Isabelle leveled her with a stare. "I'm not making excuses. I'm just trying to understand. He apologized. And I know I shouldn't take him back." Isabelle stopped pacing and dropped her hands. "You guys, I really think he might have changed this time."

Vivi scoffed and looked away. How could the smartest person in the entire school be so ridiculously stupid when it came to guys?

"It's just that I've always imagined going to the prom with him," Isabelle said, slumping down next to Vivi on the window seat. "Getting all dressed up and dancing with him—"

"Just because you imagined it that way, that doesn't mean it's how it's *supposed* to be," Vivi said firmly, turning to face Isabelle. "You're supposed to be with a guy who loves you. A guy who *respects* you."

Isabelle's face fell. "I *know* he loves me."

"But he doesn't respect you," Lane piped in quietly from the bed.

Vivi and Isabelle looked over at her. She'd been so silent for the past few minutes, Vivi had practically forgotten she was there.

"I'm sorry, Iz, but a guy who really respects you and cares about you isn't going to hook up with some girl behind your back," Lane said calmly. "And he wasn't even discreet about it. But even if he was, it wouldn't make it okay."

"You guys—"

"She's right, Iz," Vivi said, buoyed by Lane's backup. "There are other guys out there. Great guys. Guys who won't cheat on you and just expect you to take them back. Guys like—"

Lane's eyes widened, and Vivi snapped her mouth shut. She couldn't believe the word that was on the tip of her tongue. Had she really been about to mention Brandon?

"Guys like who?" Isabelle asked.

"I don't know! Like—"

Something in the room beeped. Isabelle got up and walked closer to her computer. There was an IM screen dead in the center. Vivi, Lane, and Isabelle all leaned toward it to see. Vivi's heart caught in her throat when she read the message.

Brandon: Hey, Izzy. What's up?

Vivi looked at Lane, livid. What the hell was Marshall doing? What if he flipped into his default dork setting and started going on about how Batman is the only true super-hero or something?

Oh, Marshmallow, you are so very dead, Vivi thought, fuming.

"Uh . . . who's that?" Lane asked finally, with a too-calm voice.

"Oh . . . uh . . . no one," Isabelle said quickly, bringing up her New York Liberty screen saver. "Just someone I met online." Her cheeks turned a little pink, and she bit her lip to keep from grinning. Vivi's heart started to pitter-patter in her chest. It was working!

"No one, huh? Then why are you blushing?" Vivi teased, nudging Isabelle with her arm. As irritated as she was at Marshall right then, she was ecstatic to see Isabelle's reaction to Brandon firsthand.

"I don't know. He's . . . he's sweet. But it's nothing. I mean, it's ridiculous," Isabelle said, lifting her hair off the back of her neck as if she were overheating just thinking about it. "We've just been talking. That's all."

"Flirting, you mean," Vivi said, moving to take charge of the mouse, as if she wanted to check out Brandon for herself.

"Well, maybe," Isabelle admitted with a shrug, letting the grin finally come through. In the same move, she swooped in and stood between the computer and Vivi.

"You're totally crushing on him!" Lane announced, looking amazed.

"That's insane. We met on*line.*" There was another beep, and Isabelle flinched. "I'd better write back. Give me a sec."

She pulled out her chair and sat down, forcing Vivi to back up a step, but she managed to hover close enough to be able to see what Izzy and Marshall were typing.

> **IzzyBelly:** Busy just now. Sorry. Can I IM you later?
> **Brandon:** Definitely. Just wanted to ask how the prom stuff is progressing. Found anyone worthy?

Isabelle giggled before replying. Vivi held her breath to see what she would say.

> **IzzyBelly:** Still working on it. Will keep you posted.

No mention of Shawn. That had to mean something— Isabelle wasn't telling her online crush about her potential date with her ex. It had to mean that part of her was still hoping for something better—that there was still a possibility they could fix this. But how?

Isabelle brought up her screen saver again and stood. "What were we talking about?" she asked, all goofy.

"The prom," Lane supplied, with a huge grin.

"Oh. Right," Isabelle shook her head and looked toward the window, still smiling. She was still giddy over just four lines between her and Brandon. The last thing Vivi wanted to do now was steer the conversation back to prom and Shawn and away from Izzy's new crush.

"Look at you. I haven't seen you like this since you got Dwayne Wade's autograph," Vivi said happily. "This Brandon kid makes you as giddy as Dwayne does."

Isabelle laughed and crossed her arms over her chest. "Ha-ha. Too bad I can't take *him* to the prom."

Vivi felt as if someone had just dumped a bucket of ice water over her head. Every single nerve in her body tingled. How had she not thought of this before?

"Hey, Iz? I'm kinda hungry. Can Lane and I go raid the fridge?" Vivi blurted, her voice unusually loud. Lane looked at Vivi quizzically and then quickly covered it up when Izzy looked at her.

"Sure," Izzy said with a shrug. "I think there's still some sandwiches left over from the fund-raiser my parents hosted the other night."

"Perfect!" Vivi said with a grin, yanking on Lane's arm.

The second they were through the door, Vivi pulled Lane's arm hard and dragged her down the hallway.

"Ow! Vivi! What the heck?" Lane said, wrenching free from Vivi's grip.

"I just had the most brilliant idea!" Vivi whispered furtively.

Lane took one look at her, and her shoulders slumped. "Why do I have a bad feeling about this?"

"Don't! I'm telling you! It's the most genius, brilliant, perfect idea I have ever had!" Vivi promised her. "Even you are not going to be able to deny my genius."

Lane took a deep breath. "All right," she said reluctantly. "Lay it on me."

★ ★ ★ ★ *six* ★ ★ ★ ★

"You have *got* to be kidding me!" Lane cried an hour later, sitting in the passenger's seat of Vivi's convertible Jetta. It was a beautiful, sunny spring afternoon. Kids played hopscotch in their driveways, moms speed-walked along the sidewalks, a pack of middle school boys did tricks on their dirt bikes in the deserted parking lot of the old roller rink. It was the kind of day on which Lane would have normally enjoyed tooling around with the top down, reveling in the quaintness of her town. Unfortunately, Vivi and her insanity were making that virtually impossible. "You really want to hire some guy to play Brandon and take Isabelle to the prom?"

"Why not? It's perfect!" Vivi replied, her blond hair whipping around her head as she drove. "Brandon is perfect for her. What better way to get her mind off Shawn than to set her up with her perfect guy?"

Lane stared at her Vivi. Had she finally cracked? One too many schemes, and she'd crossed the line into total delusion.

"Yeah. One problem. Brandon doesn't actually exist!" Lane's voice rose with each word as she held her own hair back from her head so that it would stop hitting her in the eye.

"So? We didn't post a picture. We could get anyone to play him!" Vivi said easily.

"Right. And where are we going to find a guy our age who'd be willing to go to our prom? Oh, and who Isabelle has never met?" Lane asked as Vivi turned onto her tree-lined street.

"At another school," Vivi replied, lifting a hand off the wheel. Like it was so obvious.

"And how, exactly, are we going to get him to pretend he's some fictional guy named Brandon?" Lane asked, using one hand to hold her hair back and the other to shield the glare of the afternoon sun.

"We'll pay him!" Vivi said.

"With what?"

"I still have money left over from lifeguarding last summer," Vivi told her. "It's gotta be enough to buy one prom date."

"Come on. What kind of guy would do this for a little money?" Lane asked.

Vivi gave her a sidelong glance. "Please. Look at Curtis! What would that boy *not* do for some extra Xbox cash?"

Lane sighed in consternation. Curtis had once babysat his next-door neighbor's twin two-year-old girls for an entire

Saturday just so he could get the new Tony Hawk game. He'd come home with a chunk cut out of his hair, applesauce up his nose, and permanent purple marker slashes all over his arms, but had claimed it was totally worth it.

"Okay, but once we find a guy, he's going to have to learn everything we made up about Brandon," Lane said as Vivi stopped her car in front of Lane's house. "How are we going to teach him all that?"

"Please. The prom is almost three weeks away!" Vivi said happily, turning to face Lane as the car idled. "We have plenty of time. Besides, Curtis can help. It might be good to spend as much time with him as possible right now," Vivi wheedled, looking sly. "Maybe plant some seeds about what a perfect prom date you'd make . . . ?"

Lane leaned her head back on the leather seat and groaned. Why did Vivi have to be so damn persistent? And why, why, why did she always have to suck Lane into her plans? As if Lane didn't have enough to deal with in her own life. Although, the idea of bringing Curtis in did make it slightly more appealing . . .

"Come on, Laney," Vivi pleaded. "We can*not* let Isabelle go to the prom with Shawn. It'll be her sweet sixteen all over again!"

A lump formed in Lane's throat at the very memory. Isabelle's sweet sixteen was supposed to be the party of the year, and Shawn was supposed to play an integral role. Back then, when Izzy's parents weren't as familiar with Shawn as they were now, they had left Isabelle's new car with him, and he was supposed to drive it to the hall where the party was taking place. Unfortunately, Shawn had decided to take the auto for a joyride first and, while flipping stations on the satellite radio, had driven the thing right into the rear bumper of a student driver. Then he proceeded to tell the driving instructor off until he noticed the guy taking down the license plate number and ran off, abandoning Izzy's car in a parking lot like a coward. In the end, Shawn never showed up, the car was impounded before Isabelle ever got to see it, the police had come to the party to inform Isabelle's parents, and Izzy had ended the night in tears.

"I still can't believe she forgave him for that," Lane said, her heart heavy.

"Yeah, well, it was an 'accident'!" Vivi said facetiously, throwing in some air quotes. "All he had to do was make himself the victim and, presto, instant forgiveness."

Lane looked down at her hands. As insane as Vivi's plan was, it was preferable to seeing Isabelle that heartbroken all over again.

Lane sighed and looked at Vivi. "Okay, now let's just say I said yes—"

"Yes!" Vivi cheered, slapping her hands together.

"I haven't said it yet!" Lane blurted, avoiding Vivi's eyes and looking out the windshield. "But say that I did. Where are we going to find some perfect hottie to be Brandon?"

Vivi smiled slowly and Lane's heart sank. She should have known the girl would have an answer for everything.

"Where do all the most perfect boys in the tri-state area go to school?"

Lane, suddenly, found herself smiling as well. Vivi *was* brilliant.

"Saint Paul's Prep."

* * *

Vivi slammed open her bedroom door. Marshall was so startled, he jumped up from her computer and knocked over her chair.

"Omigod! Are you *still* talking to her?" Vivi demanded, walking across to the computer screen. Marshall reached for the mouse to try to close the window, but Vivi was too fast. She snatched it away, and he backed up a few steps. Sure enough, there was an IM window open, and Isabelle was typing a response. "You are unbelievable!" Vivi shouted at Marshall. "You can't write to her when I'm not here!"

Marshall's mouth opened and closed a few times as he struggled for words. "How did you—?"

"We were at her house when a message from Brandon suddenly popped up," Vivi said, pulling her Rutgers sweatshirt off over her head as she tugged down on the black T-shirt underneath. "I was so surprised, I almost freaked out and gave the whole thing away."

Marshall shoved his hands into his armpits. "Did you . . . uh . . . see what we were writing?"

"That is not the point! I'm *supposed* to see what you're writing," Vivi blurted. She crouched down to set her chair up again. "You cannot write to her without me here!"

"Why not?" Marshall asked.

"Because! What if you . . . I don't know . . . said something that contradicted what we made up?" Vivi asked, yanking her ponytail out and then smoothing her hair back to retie it.

Marshall followed her with his eyes as she paced across the room, his expression doubtful. "It's not that much, and it's all on his page," he said. "I think I can figure it out."

"Don't you have anything better to do than talk to my best friend as a fictional character?" Vivi asked, whirling on him. Then she thought about it for half a second. "Never mind—I know the answer."

"You're the one who asked for my help with this thing," Marshall said, indignant. He grabbed his soda can from her desk and headed for the door. "If you don't like the way I do it, then maybe I'll just not do it anymore."

"No!" Vivi blurted, panicking. "You can't quit now."

Marshall paused and looked at her, eyebrows raised. "Why not?"

"Well, we don't want her to think you've lost interest," Vivi said, cursing herself for having to plead with Marshall. "You have to keep it up—at least until we find somebody to play Brandon."

"Play Brandon?" Marshall asked, suddenly looking a little pale.

"Yeah. We're gonna hire someone to pretend he's him and take Isabelle to the prom," Vivi explained quickly, grabbing a brush from her dresser and pulling it quickly though her hair. "You know, so she doesn't go with Sluttig."

Marshall's jaw dropped, and he walked over to Vivi's

dresser. "Are you out of your mind? You're going to set your best friend up with a fake prom date?"

"He's gonna be a real guy," Vivi retorted, swinging her hair to her other shoulder to brush out the ends. "It's not like I'm building a robot or something."

"You may as well be!" Marshall said, putting his soda down on the wood. "Where are you going to find this person?"

Vivi's nerves started to sizzle, and she slammed the brush back down. "Coaster, loser?" She practically tossed the soda can back to Marshall and quickly checked for a water stain. "I don't know. Around," she replied. "We're thinking about going to Saint Paul's Prep, actually."

Marshall let out an indignant noise that only irritated her more. "So you're just gonna pick up some guy off the street? What if he turns out to be a psycho killer or something?"

"Dude, you've read too many Hannibal Lecter novels," Vivi replied, tying her hair back again. "You don't think I'm smart enough not to hire some crazy person?"

"No. No way." Marshall turned and walked out the door. "I can't do this. Helping her get over a breakup is one thing, but hiring guys to take her out? That's way too pimplike for me."

Vivi jogged out her door and followed him down the hall to his room. On the way, she couldn't help noticing his jeans. His brand-new, dark-wash, kind-of-distressed, and totally cool jeans.

"Hey, where did you get those?" Vivi asked, pointing as she leaned into his doorjamb.

Marshall looked down. "The mall," he said. "Now would you please leave me alone?"

Part of Vivi wanted to grill Marshall a bit more about all these random changes. The new hair, the new jeans, the toned arms. But she had more important details to focus on.

"No. I won't," Vivi protested. "Come on, Marshall. You can't quit now! What're you gonna do? Break up with her?"

Marshall flung himself down on his bed and raised his hands to his temples like he had a splitting headache. "I don't have to break up with her. You can talk to her from now on."

Vivi considered this a moment, but knew it would never work. She could never sound like Marshall if she tried.

"No I can't. You've already set up a whole relationship with her. I don't know what you guys talk about. What if she references something you said and I have no clue? Besides, I don't have time now. I have to find a guy and teach him to be Brandon!"

"Vivi—"

"Marshall, you're the one who's got her all gooey over there. You can't just quit on us now," Vivi begged, leaning one hand against the doorjamb.

"I do?" Marshall asked, lifting his head.

"You do what?" Vivi asked, confused.

"Have her all gooey?" he asked. "It's actually working?"

Vivi rolled her eyes and threw her hands up. "Yeah. Congratulations! You're a virtual Romeo. And if you bail now, she'll be heartbroken all over again. Not that you care."

Marshall sat up straight, crossing his legs. He knocked his fist against his knee a few times and smiled. "Fine. I'll do it," he said finally, looking a little nervous.

"Yes!" Vivi cheered, dancing around a little in the doorway. "Thank you."

She ran over to the bed and hugged him quickly, but he pushed her back to look her in the eye. "But in thirty years when I'm forced to commit you to a mental asylum, I don't want a hard time," he said.

Vivi laughed and then raised her right hand. "I promise."

★ ★ ★ seven ★ ★ ★

"I'm in," Curtis said with a nod, standing outside Westmont High the next day.

Lane's jaw dropped slightly. "You're in. Just like that. You have no problem with this totally insane plan, and you want to come with us to Saint Paul's right now to pick up guys."

"Why not? It's for Isabelle, right?" Curtis asked with a shrug. He slipped his Oakleys on and started down the hill toward the parking lot. Lane and Vivi exchanged a surprised and amused look.

"Curtis, are you gay?" Vivi asked, as they jogged to catch up with him.

"Vivi!" Lane said with a laugh.

"Um, no. But out of curiosity, why do you ask?" Curtis said.

"What? It would just explain so much," Vivi explained. "Your willingness to come with us to scope guys, the fact that you've never had a girlfriend, the fact that you don't yet have a *prom date,*" she said pointedly.

Lane blushed and looked at the ground. Could Vivi be any less subtle?

"One, I'm just helping you with your plan," Curtis said, holding up a finger. "Two, I've never had a girlfriend because I have very high standards, and three, I don't see either one of you guys rocking a prom date either."

Vivi frowned quickly. "Hmm. True."

They arrived at Vivi's Jetta, and Curtis jumped over the side into the backseat. "Ow. Damn. Could you keep any more crap back here, Vivi?"

He pulled a bottle of gel out from under his butt and tossed it on the floor at his feet.

"Back off, Mr. High Standards. I don't tell you how to keep your car," Vivi said, getting in behind the wheel and tossing her blond hair over her shoulder.

"That's because I don't have a car. But if I did, you would," Curtis pointed out, taking a long swig from his water bottle.

Lane laughed as she handed him the blank canvas she was bringing home for a new painting, and he placed it carefully next to him in the backseat.

"So, what's the plan again?" Lane asked as she got in the car. Her chest felt tight, and her palms were already starting to sweat. She could hardly get up the guts to talk to the guys at her own school—guys she'd known since kindergarten— let alone the thought of all the perfect Saint Paul's Prep boys and their perfection.

"It'll take about twenty minutes to get there, so we should

catch a bunch of them on their way out of practices and club meetings," Vivi said, starting the car. "Grab the first cute guy you see, tell him you have an incredible proposition for him, and then just sell it."

Lane nodded and took a deep breath. "Just sell it."

"You okay?" Vivi asked, looking over at Lane as she buckled her seat belt. "You look a little pale."

"I'm fine." Lane propped her elbow up on the top of the car door. "Let's just get this over with."

"You got it!"

Vivi whipped her car out of its space. They sat in the bottleneck of traffic near the parking lot exit for a few minutes, and Curtis started drumming his hands on the backs of their seats. Lane saw Vivi's hands tightening on the steering wheel and knew her friend was about five seconds from totally flipping out on him.

"So no basketball today?" Lane asked Curtis, turning around in her seat to look at him. She had to shade her eyes from the glare of the sun.

"They're playing, but I'm sick of it. Jeff's way too competitive. Did you see that black eye Lewis Richards had today?" Curtis asked, sitting forward and propping his forearms on his knees.

"Yeah. So nasty," Lane said.

"That was all Jeff and his flagrant fouls," Curtis replied, leaning back suddenly as if exasperated. "I like my face the way it is, thank you very much."

So do I, Lane thought, pulling her hair over her shoulder and facing front again so Curtis couldn't see her blush.

"So, Curtis, really. Why haven't you asked anyone to the prom yet?" Vivi asked out of nowhere.

"God! TFP!" Curtis groaned.

"Curtis!" Vivi scolded.

"Sorry! The freaking prom!" Curtis amended. "It's all anyone's talking about. Like there's nothing else going on in the world. What I wouldn't give for one good conversation about global warming," he joked. He crossed his arms and looked out the side of the car. "Do either of you know who you want to go with?"

"No," Lane said. Her heart was going to give up on her. It had to. It could not keep up this insane rhythm.

"I'm thinking about going stag," Vivi said.

"Really?" Lane asked, looking over at Vivi. That was news to her.

"That's brave," Curtis added.

"Yeah, well, our school is devoid of datable guys," Vivi said, turning onto Essex Road, the wide thoroughfare that connected Westmont to the next few towns. "And I definitely don't want to babysit some random setup date all night."

"Exactly! I want to go with someone cool, you know? Someone who'll just be able to kick back and have fun and not take the whole thing so seriously," Curtis said.

What about me? Lane thought, her heart pounding. *I can kick back and have fun!*

"Anyone in mind?" Vivi asked, looking at Lane out of the corner of her eye. Lane squirmed, wishing she could be anywhere but here right now. Why couldn't Vivi just leave it alone?

"Well, there's this one girl ...," Curtis said. "But I don't know. I doubt she'd ever go with me."

Vivi looked uncertainly, pityingly, at Lane. Lane felt like the whole world had just stopped as the trees and mailboxes continued to whip past her. Like she wasn't even really there. Curtis had a date in mind. He liked someone. Someone he saw as unattainable. In other words, not her. Not Lane. Of course he wasn't thinking of Lane. Why would he? She was his friend. His neighbor. Literally, the girl next door. The girl who walked his bike home from school. Why did she ever let herself think for even a second that he might see her as anything more?

"Who is she?" Vivi demanded.

"No one you know," Curtis replied.

I'm going to throw up, Lane thought, checking the junk near her feet for something that could double as a barf bag.

"Come on. Who is she?" Vivi wheedled, probably figuring Lane would want to know. Well, Vivi was wrong about that. Lane would rather tear her eardrums out than talk about Curtis's dream date.

"Vivi, he doesn't want to tell us. Drop it," Lane said quietly.

Vivi took one look at Lane's pallor and bit her tongue. "Fine," she grumbled.

"Okay! So! New topic!" Curtis announced, oblivious. "So what, exactly, are we looking for in a Brandon?"

Vivi filled Curtis in, babbling on and on about hotness factor and smoldering qualities. Lane, meanwhile, stared out the window, trying to get control of her breathing.

It's over. He doesn't want you, she told herself, trying to accept it. *At least now you know, and you can move on.* But her logic didn't make her heart hurt any less, and it didn't make the unshed tears recede from her eyes.

Somehow, the not knowing had been a whole lot better.

"Eh. She's not that hot," Toothy Blond Dude said to Vivi, giving Isabelle's picture a cursory glance. He wore the standard Saint Paul's Prep uniform—light blue shirt, burgundy-and-blue plaid tie, and burgundy jacket over tan pants. But since it was after hours, the tie was loosened and the shirt was untucked. Vivi had thought he looked pretty sexy, until he blew off her perfectly gorgeous best friend as if she were a troll. "Now *you* on the other hand . . . ," he added, looking Vivi up and down.

Vivi rolled her eyes impatiently. What was it about attending an ancient school with all-brick buildings and no estrogen to speak of that turned guys into egomaniacs? She saw over his shoulder that Curtis and Lane had reconvened on a bench in the center of the sun-drenched quad. Neither of them looked particularly happy.

"*I*, on the other hand, have a black belt in karate," Vivi lied, stepping slightly away from the swiftly advancing guy. "So if you have any interest in retaining your ability to procreate, you'll walk away right now."

Toothy Blond Dude made a disgusted face and walked away. "Freak."

"Loser," she called out loudly. Then she pocketed her

Isabelle picture and walked off to join her friends. "No luck?" she asked, dropping down on Curtis's right.

"Nothing. All the guys I talked to either thought I was in some cult or thought I was punking them or something," Lane said, slouching far down onto the bench.

"I figured her picture would seal the deal, but they all thought I was showing them a fake. Like there's no way a girl as pretty as Isabelle can't get a date to the prom." Curtis sighed, dejected. "Which, of course, makes sense."

"This is ridiculous," Vivi said, scuffing her sneakers into the dirt at the base of the bench. "We have to find somebody." She spotted a pair of tall basketball-player types strolling along the path toward the parking lot and nodded in their direction. "What about them?"

"Too scrawny," Curtis replied. "Shawn's a big guy."

"Him?" Lane asked, pointing to a kid who was bobbing his head to his iPod as he walked.

"No chin," Curtis put in.

"Wait a minute! I think we have a winner!" Vivi announced, straightening up a little.

Coming toward them on the pathway was a tall, broad guy with shaggy blond hair—just like Shawn's. He was rocking a killer tan early in the season, so he was probably one of those privileged guys who got to vacation with his parents in the Caribbean all the time. Or skiing in Aspen. He was chatting with a teacher as they walked together, and he carried himself with total confidence.

"Now *he's* hot," Curtis said, sitting up straight.

Vivi and Lane both looked at Curtis in amusement.

"What? I'm just totally secure with my sexuality," he said. "Secure enough to be able to say that guy is physically worthy of Isabelle."

Lane and Vivi cracked up laughing. The boy in question was getting closer.

"All right. I'm on it," Vivi said, standing up.

God, he was even hotter up close. His eyes were like aquamarines. She was just about to reach out and interrupt the conversation when the guy laughed at something the teacher had said. Cackled, actually. Exploding all over the place like a rabid hyena. He doubled over at the waist right in front of Lane and sucked in air with wheezing gasps. Vivi backed up a step, worried he might have a seizure or something. It was the most awful noise she had ever heard.

When he finally stood up again and started walking, still struggling for air, Vivi was still too stunned to speak. But as he passed her by, she got a very up close and personal look at his "Caribbean tan." It was practically orange. She looked at her friends, baffled.

"Was he wearing makeup?" Curtis asked gleefully.

"I think it was a spray-on tan," Lane replied. "How superficial can you be?"

"Okay, that was scary," Vivi said, picking up her messenger bag. "Let's get the heck out of here. This school sucks. I have lost all respect for the Saint Paul's Prep mystique."

"Yeah. These guys are not that hot," Lane agreed, standing as well.

"Well, they are hot, but they still suck," Vivi amended. "Come on. Let's go get something to eat and regroup."

✳ ✳ ✳

"This is good pizza," Marshall said brightly, gnawing away on his third slice of pepperoni.

"Glad you like it. You owe us six bucks," Vivi grumbled. She crumpled her napkin and tossed it into the open pizza box on the kitchen table. Upstairs, Vivi heard her mother corner Curtis on his way back from the bathroom, chatting with him about the open call the Starlight was holding for their production of *Bye Bye Birdie*.

"Mom! Leave him alone! He doesn't want to be in your musical!" Vivi shouted, tipping her head back.

"We're just talking, sweetie!" Vivi's mother trilled.

She did, however, release poor Curtis, who rejoined them seconds later. "Your mother is TTF."

"Yeah, right," Vivi replied, taking a sip of Pepsi. At least she knew that TTF was "totally too funny." She was getting more and more accustomed to Curtis's strange language. "Sorry about that."

"She's just being Mom," Marshall said lightly, chewing his slice.

"Why are you in such a good mood?" she asked her brother.

Marshall shrugged, smiling as he chewed. "No reason. Good pizza. Good day. That's about it."

Vivi glanced at Lane across the table. Her brother was acting like he was on something. Something a bit more powerful than pepperoni and Pepsi.

"So. No Brandons at Saint Paul's Prep, huh?" Marshall

asked, reaching for his soda. "That's too bad. I mean, if you can't find a willing guy there . . ."

"He has a point, Viv," Lane said, sitting forward in her vinyl chair. "Saint Paul's is the hot guy mecca of the tri-state area. Maybe it's time to—"

Vivi threw her hand up. "Do not finish that sentence. We are not giving up. We've just had a minor setback."

Lane's posture crumbled, and she rested the side of her head in her hand. "I had a feeling you were going to say that."

"Come on, guys. Think!" Vivi said, standing up. She paced over to the shelf on the wall that held all her mother's kitschy salt and pepper shakers and toyed with them. Ceramic cacti from Arizona, a pair of glass owls, the Eiffel Tower and Notre Dame. "Where else can we find cute boys that Isabelle's never met? There has to be somewhere."

"We could try a different school," Lane suggested half-heartedly.

"Nah. If we learned anything today, it's that strangers approaching high school guys with a proposition like this is way too weird," Curtis said, gnawing on a piece of pizza crust.

"Exactly." Vivi paced at the end of the table, racking her brain. "We have to think outside the box. How else do people find dates?"

"Match-dot-com?" Marshall suggested.

"No time for that," Vivi replied. "What we need is to find a guy who would be up for anything. Someone who needs to make a quick buck. Someone who doesn't mind the idea of potentially making a fool of himself."

"Too bad we can't ask my mom for help," Lane said. "Whenever one of her famous clients needs an image boost, she just holds a go-see and picks out some hot model for him to go out with and be photographed with. She'd be able to find us a Brandon in less than an hour."

"What's a go-see?" Vivi asked, leaning back on the kitchen counter.

"It's like an audition," Lane said. "Except the models just come in and show their portfolios and strut around. It sounds totally shallow to me, but—"

"Wait a minute, what did you just say?" Vivi asked, her skin prickling with heat.

Lane stared at her. "I said it sounds totally shallow to me, but—"

"No! Not that part. An audition! That's perfect!" Vivi cried, slapping Notre Dame back on the shelf.

"You want to hold an audition," Lane said flatly. "Are you kidding me? How would we get people to come without Isabelle hearing about it?"

"We don't have to get people to come," Curtis said, pushing himself away from the wall, his brown eyes sparkling. "We already know someone who's holding an open call."

Vivi grinned at Curtis.

"You guys," Marshall said warily. "You're not thinking what I think you're thinking, are you?"

"Mom!" Vivi shouted at the top of her lungs. She turned and jogged to the bottom of the stairs.

"Omigod! It's perfect!" Lane said, finally catching on. She

got up and she, Curtis, and Marshall followed Vivi, crowding around her in the entryway.

"Vivi! What in the world?" her mother asked, appearing at the top of the steps.

"Sorry!" Vivi said, bounding up the stairs. She took her mother's arm and practically dragged her back down to the foyer. "I'm just so excited about your auditions. You're doing *Bye Bye Birdie*, right?"

"Right . . . ," her mother said, confused. She looked around at all the eager faces and seemed slightly disturbed.

"There's a lot of teenagers in that, right?" Curtis leaned on the stair railing.

"We are looking for some younger cast members," Vivi's mom said. Then her eyes sparkled with excitement. "Have you changed your mind about auditioning, Curtis? Because that would be—"

"No, Mom. We were just wondering . . . can we come to the auditions with you on Monday? Me and Lane and Curtis? Just to watch."

Vivi's mother was stunned. "Come with me? Why?"

"I don't know. I'm just . . . I'm just dying to see how the whole thing works," Vivi improvised, grasping her mother's hand and walking back into the kitchen. "I mean, it's your job! Your passion! I want to share it with you!"

Marshall shook his head, dropping back into his chair at the table.

"But, Vivi. You've never expressed an interest in musical theater before!" Vivi's mother pointed out, breathless with surprise.

"Oh, please! You are so wrong!" Vivi protested. "Mom, theater is my life!"

Marshall crossed his arms on the table and dropped his head down.

"Oh, Vivi! You have no idea how much it means to me to hear you say that!" her mother said, tears springing to her eyes.

Vivi flashed Lane and Curtis a thumbs-up as her mother hugged her happily. At the table, Marshall groaned.

"I'm going to call the casting director right now!" Vivi's mother announced. "She's going to be so excited you kids are coming!"

She floated out of the room, and Vivi basked in her triumph. "Theater geeks! Why didn't we think of this before?"

"It's too perfect," Curtis said, beaming.

"And we don't even have to go up to any of them," Lane put in, obviously relieved. "They'll be up on stage auditioning for us."

"For Mom," Marshall said, looking a little green. "They're going to be auditioning for Mom. Who, by the way, you just completely snowed," he said to Vivi.

"Dude. Chill out. She's happy—I'm happy. It's a win–win!" Vivi said, grabbing another slice of pepperoni off the counter. "By this time next week, we'll have our Brandon."

"I just wish we didn't have to wait until Monday," Lane said. "What if Shawn convinces Isabelle to go to the prom with him before then?"

"We'll just have to keep her away from him until then. Marshall will step up the lovey-dovey talk online, and we'll keep her occupied," Vivi said. "If she hasn't said yes to him yet, it has to be because of Brandon. We just have to keep it going."

"So you're using our mother—by toying with her fondest dream, by the way—so that you can hire a fake prom date for your best friend, who has no idea any of this is going on," Marshall said, staring up at her. "You're going to hell, you know that, don't you?"

Vivi smiled. "Yeah, but it's gonna be a fun ride."

eight

Lane stared at herself in the full-length mirror of her dressing room. This was it. This was the dress. After trying on two dozen different gowns, she had thought she would never find it, but this was definitely the one. The light blue color brought out her eyes, but didn't make her skin look too pink, as so many other dresses had. And she loved the way the lace scalloped at the top. With the little ribbon belt and the full tea-length skirt, it was both pretty and trendy. Perfect.

"You guys! Come out already!" Vivi shouted from the little sitting room outside. "What's taking so long?"

"All right! I'm coming," Lane replied.

"Me too!" Isabelle added.

Lane stepped into the common area of the dressing room, and Vivi and her mother both stood up. Vivi was still wearing the dress she had picked—a sophisticated floor-length black gown with a halter top that tied behind her neck—and both she and her mom covered their mouths with their hands when they saw Lane.

"Honey. That dress is perfect on you," Vivi's mother said.

Lane beamed. "I know. Now I just have to call my mom and get her to agree to spend double what she said." The very thought took the smile right off her face.

"Let me call her. I can be very convincing," Vivi's mother offered. She pulled out her cell and stepped out of the room.

"I love it," Vivi told Lane. "Seriously. It's perfect."

"Thanks." They both turned to look for Isabelle, who had yet to emerge from her dressing room. "Iz?" Lane called.

Silence. Vivi's brow creased in concern, and she walked over to the room. "Isabelle? Are you okay?"

"M'fine," Isabelle replied tearily.

"Oh God." Vivi shoved open the door, and there stood Isabelle in what could only be described as her dream dress. It was her signature powder pink with a skinny waist and a slim skirt—just like the dresses she had been admiring in magazines for years. Lane could just imagine her standing up on stage, beaming with pride as the prom queen crown everyone knew she was going to win was placed atop her perfect hair. But right then, Izzy was staring at her reflection with miserable tears in her eyes.

"Isabelle! It's beautiful!" Lane searched around for something Izzy could use as a tissue. "What's wrong?"

"I don't have a date!" Isabelle cried. She collapsed onto the little upholstered seat in her dressing room. "It's a perfect, beautiful dress and I have no one to wear it for!"

"So wear it for yourself!" Vivi said.

"No. This is wrong. I'm calling Shawn." Isabelle dove for her purse and started digging though it. "We have to go together. He knows we have to go together."

"No!" Lane blurted. Before she even knew what she was doing, she had grabbed the strap of Isabelle's purse and yanked it away.

"Lane! Give it back! It's my decision," Isabelle said, advancing on her.

Lane shoved the bag at Vivi, who was much stronger and faster than she was. "Isabelle, no," Lane said, holding out a hand. "You are not thinking clearly right now. You are under the influence of the dress."

"No, I'm not! In fact, I'm thinking clearly for the first time!" Isabelle ranted. "I mean, what am I waiting for? Some guy on the Internet to tell me that he loves our conversations so much, he's going to drive two and a half hours to take me to the prom? Ha! Like that's ever going to happen."

Lane looked at Vivi, nonplussed. So the plan really was working. She really did want to go to the prom with Brandon. She just didn't think it was a possibility.

"Besides, I love Shawn. I know he's not perfect, but I love him. I can't help it. Why shouldn't I go to the prom with him?" Isabelle asked, twirling her little silver ring around on her finger. She suddenly made a grab for her purse, but Vivi held it out of her reach.

"Because he'll ruin it!" Lane blurted. "Just like he ruins everything for you!"

Isabelle looked at Lane, her bottom lip trembling.

"I'm sorry, Iz, but it's true. Look at yourself." She turned Isabelle so she could see herself in the mirror. "You look beautiful even without the makeup and the hair and the jewelry. Now imagine yourself all done up, waiting at your house all excited. And waiting. And waiting. Because he never shows up. Or he shows up drunk and acts like a jerk the whole night. Just imagine how you'll feel then."

Isabelle took a deep breath. Lane held on to her arms from behind. She and Vivi stared at each other in the mirror, hoping that this would work. For the first time, Lane truly thought that a fake Brandon was the best alternative for her friend. It had to be better than Shawn.

"Fine," Isabelle said finally, slumping.

"Good. Good decision," Lane said, releasing Izzy.

Isabelle smoothed down the front of her dress and squared her shoulders. "I didn't say I was definitely not going with him, though. I'm just not calling him right now," she cautioned.

"But Isabelle," Vivi said. "I—"

"I don't want to talk about it anymore," Isabelle said determinedly, standing up and advancing toward Vivi and Lane. "I'm getting changed."

Izzy closed the door on her friends, and Lane took a deep breath. Vivi pulled her aside, far enough away from Isabelle's cubicle to go unheard.

"What are we going to do? She's about to crack!" Vivi whispered.

"At least we stopped her for now. One step at a time," Lane told her. "And tomorrow, we'll find our Brandon. No matter how many bad renditions of 'Put on a Happy Face' we have to sit through."

Vivi's brow creased. "'Put on a Happy Face'?"

"It's from *Bye Bye Birdie*. I did my research," Lane told her, slapping her hand down on Vivi's bare shoulder. "We are *so* in for it."

★ ★ ★ ★ nine ★ ★ ★ ★

"Okay, now I know why your mom was so desperate to have me audition for this thing," Curtis said, putting his feet up on the seat in front of him. On the stage, a man with salt-and-pepper hair crooned his way through "Put on a Happy Face," which, as Lane predicted, Vivi had already heard *way* too many times today. "I thought this show was about teenagers. This guy is, like, geriatric."

"There are some older roles in the show," Lane whispered. "Mr. MacAfee . . . Albert Peterson . . . Ed Sullivan . . ."

Curtis looked at her, and then at Vivi, who rolled her eyes. "She did research," Vivi said facetiously.

"Hey! I like to be prepared!" Lane sulked.

Curtis patted her on the head. "We know. It's what we love about you."

And, of course, Lane blushed like a madwoman.

Mr. Geriatric finally finished his song and walked off stage.

95

Vivi took a deep, calming breath and adjusted her position in her seriously uncomfortable theater seat. The Starlight Playhouse, where her mother spent most of her waking hours, was an old, airy theater with gilded box seats and a huge balcony that seemed like it hadn't been renovated since the dawn of time. Although the décor was beautifully old school, with its carvings and elaborate tapestries, there were loose springs in every seat and the distinct scent of rotting wood in the air. Still, they put on some of the most acclaimed regional shows in all of New Jersey each year. Or so her mother was always telling her.

"Oooh. What about him?" Lane asked suddenly, sitting up straight.

A tall guy with broad shoulders and dark hair strode out on stage. He wore a black T-shirt and jeans and looked to be two or three years older than Isabelle, but that wasn't too bad. "Possibly . . . ," Vivi said.

Then he sniffed back some phlegm, reached down and adjusted himself, and spoke. "Yeah. I'm auditionin' for da parda—" He looked down at his script. "—Conrad? That's a main part, right? 'Cuz I don' take no bit roles no more."

"Or not!" Vivi blurted as Lane slapped her hand over her mouth.

"Unless you want Isabelle to get whacked on prom night," Curtis joked.

"Ugh. I guess the end of *The Sopranos* put a lot of people out of work," Vivi said with a grimace.

"Ew. Ew!" Lane said, turning her face away as he sucked back more phlegm. "That is just so wrong."

As the guy performed his solo—sounding like a bad Elvis impersonator—Vivi tried to think happy thoughts. They were going to find a Brandon. Isabelle was going to be happy. The prom was going to be tons and tons of fun. . . .

"Thank you, Rocco!" Vivi's mother called out from a few rows ahead, where she was sitting with Jeannie, the director.

"He's done. You guys can open your eyes," Curtis told them.

Vivi did as she was told, but ten minutes later, she wished she hadn't. Rocco was followed by Paul of the three chins.

"He looks like he swallowed an accordion," Lane said, which sent Vivi into laughter convulsions and earned her an admonishing look from her mother.

Paul was followed by a guy named Rajeesh who cartwheeled his way on and off stage.

"We need to make a pact right now: no circus performers," Vivi said, putting her feet up on the back of the seat in front of her.

"Unless it's a bearded lady. 'Cuz that would just be fun," Curtis put in.

And Rajeesh was followed by Danny, who looked to be about twelve. He had blond hair, a pair of candy apples for cheeks, and a neck like a pencil. Vivi tipped her head back and groaned at the cracked ceiling above. "This is not working."

"Name, please?" Vivi's mother asked.

"Uh . . . Danny Hess?" the kid said, his voice cracking.

"He's kind of cute," Lane said hopefully, scooting closer to Vivi and crossing her arms over her chest.

"Yeah, for a kindergartner," Vivi put in.

"They're too young . . . they're too old. . . . There's no pleasing you people!" Curtis joked.

"I'm auditioning for the part of Randolph?" Danny said shakily.

"The little brother," Lane explained.

"Go ahead with your song, Danny," Vivi's mother said.

Danny cleared his throat and started to sing "A Whole New World" from *Aladdin*. He started out shaky, but was actually really good. Still, the whole time he was singing, Vivi's foot was bouncing up and down.

"Okay, okay. Get the kid offstage so we can get on with this!" she hissed.

Finally, Danny finished his verse and someone in the theater started to hoot and applaud. "Yeah, Danny! Whoooo!"

Startled, Vivi turned around, along with every other person in the auditorium. Standing in the very back, clapping his hands loudly, was a guy who must have been Danny's brother. He had to be, because he was basically an older, taller, broader version of Danny himself. Instantly, Vivi sat up. This guy was hot. Blond hair. Perfectly chiseled face. He was a bit preppy to be Brandon, in his rugby shirt and clean jeans, but that could be rectified. All Vivi cared about was the fact that looking at this guy was making her heart pound, and it was the first time that had happened all day.

"Well. What do we have here?" she said under her breath.

"Sorry." The guy stopped clapping and raised an apologetic hand toward Vivi's mom and her colleague. "Just . . .

trying to be supportive." He grinned in a totally endearing way. "I'll just go backstage now and wait." Then he grabbed a blue-and-yellow varsity jacket off the chair in front of him and fled.

"Sorry," Danny said from the stage, purple from neck to temple. "My brother's kind of . . . um . . . loud."

"That's all right, Danny," Vivi's mother said, smiling warmly at the boy. "We'll let you know about callbacks."

"Come on!" Vivi said, jumping out of her seat, which smacked back loudly. Her adrenaline was rushing through her veins so fast, she actually felt a bit faint.

"Where are we going?" Lane asked. She started grabbing their stuff up from the floor. "There's still an hour left."

"Not for us," Vivi hissed. "We just found our Brandon!"

✶ ✶ ✶

Vivi speed-walked along a hallway full of guys warming up their voices and going over their lines. Old guys, fat guys, skinny guys, seriously pale guys. None of them even compared to Danny Hess's brother. At least she knew that she wasn't going to be missing anything in the upcoming auditions.

"Vivi! This guy's not even an actor," Lane whispered, side-stepping a ballet dude who was stretching in a way no guy should ever stretch. "What if he can't pull it off?"

"Shut up, Lane. He's perfect," Vivi shot back.

"Wow. That was real nice," Curtis said sarcastically.

"I'm sorry, all right?" Vivi replied, glancing at them over

her shoulder. "I just don't want to miss him!"

She was just about to turn the corner toward the wings when the man himself shoved open the door to the men's bathroom and nearly took her out.

"Whoa! Watch where you're going, there!" Vivi joked.

"Sorry," the guy blurted. He started past her, but looked up as he went and paused. "Sorry," he said again.

Vivi blushed. Was that a double take he'd just done there?

Older Brother Hess was way hotter up close. His eyes were the gray blue of the Atlantic Ocean on a cloudy day, and his smile took all the air right out of her. He had a tiny white scar on the middle of his chin, and he already had a bit of a tan—not a fake one—and it was only May, which meant he was an outdoors-loving guy.

"Vivi?" Lane said as she and Curtis caught up to them.

Vivi blinked, snapping out of her trance. "You're Danny's brother, right?"

"Uh, yeah. Jonathan," he said, pulling his varsity jacket on. She wished he would turn around so she could see what school he was from and what sport he played. "Is there a problem?"

"What? Oh. No. He was great," Vivi improvised.

He smiled, and it sent shivers right through Vivi. Isabelle was going to freak for this guy.

"Great. Do you guys work here?" he asked. "Because if you do, I just want you to know if he gets the part, he'll work really hard and he'll always be on time. My parents work, but I'll drive him wherever. He really wants to be an actor for some unknown reason," he said with a laugh.

Even his laugh was sexy.

"Oh, no. We don't work here. My mother does. She's the casting director. I'm Vivi Swayne. This is Lane Morris and Curtis Miles. We're just here for . . . uh . . . fun," she said, raising her shoulders.

"Oh. Well, tell your mother I'm sorry about the outburst," Jonathan said. "I'm just proud of him, you know?" He looked around at the busy hallway, shouldering his backpack. "Where is he, anyway?"

"Oh, Curtis will go find him . . . right, Curtis?" Vivi said, turning around to beg him with her eyes.

Curtis sighed. "Yeah, yeah. I'm going." He turned and walked into the wings in search of Danny.

"So, where do you go to school?" Vivi asked Jonathan.

"Cranston Prep," Jonathan replied, turning slightly so that Vivi could see the back of his jacket. Which was, it turned out, a lacrosse jacket. She should have known. "You guys from around here?"

"We go to Westmont," Vivi replied. "Amazing, huh? We probably live fifteen minutes away from each other and have never met before. There are just way too many people in this state. Right, Lane?"

What am I saying? Vivi thought.

"Uh . . . right." Lane gave Vivi a confused look.

"So, Jonathan," Vivi said, getting ready to make her pitch. "We just—"

"Here he is!" Curtis announced, returning with Danny at his heels, all ready to go. Vivi could have strangled them both.

"Hey, thanks," Jonathan said. "Hey, great job out there!" Jonathan clasped his hand on Danny's bony little shoulder.

Danny shrugged modestly. "I did okay. They said they'd call in a couple days."

"You'll totally get it." Jonathan ruffled Danny's hair. "Well, it's been nice talking to you guys, but we should be getting back. I have an exam to study for, so . . ."

Vivi's heart pounded as he shoved open the exit door. There was absolutely no way she was letting this guy out of her sight.

"Wait! You can't go," Vivi said, running over to the exit.

Jonathan and Danny paused. "Ooookay. Why not?" Jonathan asked.

"Because . . . uh . . . we have a proposition for you," Lane said.

Jonathan looked at them, intrigued. Vivi was nearly drunk with relief. "What kind of proposition?"

"Come on. There's a diner across the street," Vivi said, pushing through the door ahead of them. "We'll buy you guys some fries and explain."

✳ ✳ ✳

Jonathan rested his wrists against the table—no elbows anywhere near the surface—and stared at Lane and Vivi. A few booths away, Curtis and Danny were wrapped up in a very serious Xbox versus PlayStation conversation that Lane knew could very well take hours. She had suggested they take their own table so that Vivi and Lane could really lay out the plan without Danny asking tons of questions—and being totally corrupted by their deviousness.

"So you want me to pretend to be some guy you made up on the Internet and take your best friend to prom so that she won't go with her boyfriend," Jonathan said flatly.

He is so *out of here,* Lane thought, glancing quickly at Vivi.

"Her *ex*-boyfriend." Vivi took a sip of her chocolate shake and placed it down on the table. "So you in?"

Jonathan sighed and leaned back into the creaky booth. "I knew I should have kept my brother away from this acting thing. Everyone in the theater business is out of their mind."

"First of all, we're not *in* the theater business," Vivi pointed out, playing with her empty straw wrapper. "And secondly, we're not crazy. If you knew what this guy was like—"

"Let me ask you this, does she want to go with him?" Jonathan said.

Vivi fell silent and huffed as she looked out the window.

"Yeah. Kind of," Lane admitted, earning a look of death from her friend.

"So why not just let her?" Jonathan asked. He grabbed a cherry tomato from his salad and popped it in his mouth. "You've gotta let people make their own mistakes, you know? You can't control your friends. If you try, it's just gonna put a strain on all your relationships."

Lane hid a laugh by shoving a French fry into her mouth. Jonathan had decoded Vivi in less time than it took for them to finish their food.

"What's with the analyzing?" Vivi said, letting her arm drop down on the table with a *smack*. "Are you a junior shrink?"

"Nah. Just taking a psych elective at school," Jonathan said with a grin. "I kind of wish my teacher were here right now, 'cuz she might bump my C to a B if she heard that little speech," he joked.

"You're getting a C and you're trying to lecture us?" Vivi shot back. "Nice try."

"Insults! Good tactic! Do you want me to help you out with this thing or not?" Jonathan asked.

Vivi glowered at him, and Lane tried not to smile. She liked this guy. It was the rare person who could actually render Vivi speechless. Still, the silence dragged on, and Lane suddenly sensed that if she didn't step in soon, Jonathan was going to bail and they'd be back to square one. And with prom less than two weeks away, square one was not an option.

"The thing is, Isabelle *has* made this mistake before. A bunch of times," Lane said calmly. "I totally understand where you're coming from. I wasn't all that psyched about this plan in the beginning either—"

Vivi mumbled something under her breath and took another long drink of her shake. She wiped her mouth with the back of her hand and glared at Lane.

"But now I think it really might be the best thing for Isabelle," Lane added. "Shawn is not a good guy, and if he keeps this up? I honestly think he might ruin her life."

Vivi glanced over at Jonathan to gauge his reaction. He seemed to be mulling it over for the first time since they'd sat down. Lane felt a little thrill inside her chest. Had she actually convinced him?

"I don't know," he said finally, playing around with the remnants of the salad with his fork. "It just seems so dishonest."

"We'll pay you," Vivi blurted.

Jonathan's eyebrows shot up, and he dropped his fork. "You're kidding."

"I've got three hundred dollars that says I'm not," Vivi told him. "Plus all expenses will be paid for. Tux, corsage, limo. Everything."

"Everything?" Lane gulped.

"Everything," Vivi replied, never taking her eyes off Jonathan. "You're gonna be driving your brother to the theater every other day for rehearsal if he gets the part, right? Three hundred dollars is a lot of gas money."

Lane smirked. Ever since Vivi had gotten her own car, she'd been complaining that all her allowance went right into the tank, and half the kids at school had part-time jobs just to pay for gas. Girl knew how to make a convincing argument.

"Yeah, but I don't know," Jonathan said. "I mean, have you guys really thought this through? What if Isabelle figures it out? Or what if someone from your school brings someone from my school to the prom and we get caught? This could be *really* messy."

Vivi sat back and crossed her arms over her chest. "You know what, Lane? I think we should bag this. This guy has no guts. There's no way this guy could be a badass like Brandon anyway." Vivi made as if to slide out of the booth.

Lane's heart skipped a surprised beat. "Vivi! What are you—?"

"Forget it, Lane. I'm done," Vivi said pointedly. She grabbed her suede jacket from the coat hook on the outside of the booth.

"Wait! I can be a badass!" Jonathan protested. "That is so not the issue. If you wanted me to be badass, I could be badass."

He pushed up the sleeves on his jacket and cracked his neck back and forth, all tough. Lane grinned. Suddenly she understood what Vivi was doing.

"See? That's not bad," Lane said.

"Oh, please. All prepped out with your lacrosse and your high moral standards and your *salad*. This is a diner, for God's sake. Who gets the garden salad?" Vivi said, zipping up her jacket like she was still going to bail. "I bet the most dangerous thing you've ever done is part your hair on the wrong side."

"Hey! I've done dangerous stuff," Jonathan replied.

"Like what?" Vivi countered. She stood next to the table with her hands on her hips.

"I snowboard," he said. "And I'm saving up for a motor-cycle."

"No way," Vivi said.

"So you *do* need money," Lane added.

Jonathan glanced away, his foot bouncing up and down under the table. He looked Lane and Vivi over, as if consider-ing whether or not they were pathological, then sighed in a resigned way. Vivi winked at Lane from the end of the table.

"All right, fine. I'll do it," he said finally.

"Yes!" Lane and Vivi cheered and Vivi sat back down.

"But right now, I do have to get my brother home." He whipped out a notebook from his backpack and scribbled something down, then tore out the page and handed it to Lane. "Here's my information. Call me and we'll figure out a time to meet."

"Thanks. We really appreciate this," Lane said, grinning widely.

"No problem. You, at least, seem like a nice girl," he said pointedly to Lane. Then he looked at Vivi and narrowed his eyes. "Jury's still out on you," he joked.

"Ha-ha," Vivi said, giving him a little smirk.

Jonathan started past the table to get his brother, but paused. "And, by the way, my hair is not parted on the wrong side."

The second he was gone, Lane and Vivi cracked up. "We did it! We found our Brandon!" Lane cheered, giving Vivi a high five.

"Isabelle is going to *love* him!" Vivi said proudly, grabbing one of Lane's fries. "Shawn Sluttig is history. Thanks to my brilliant maneuver."

"Oh my God. I can't believe he fell for that! Reverse psychology is the oldest trick in the book!" Lane said. She got up and moved to the other side of the booth, dragging her plate of food with her. Considering how wary she'd been about this plan from the start, she was surprised to find that her heart was pounding with excitement. But why not? Jonathan was gorgeous and funny and, with a little work, could definitely be Isabelle's perfect guy. Maybe Vivi had been right all along. Maybe this plan was really going to work. The very idea of Isabelle being happy and Shawn Littig–free made Lane's skin tingle.

"Well he *does* have a C in psych," Vivi joked, munching on the fries.

"So, ladies. Is Operation Skewer Sluttig a go?" Curtis asked, standing at the end of the table and rubbing his hands together. The girls cracked up.

"It's a go!" Lane cheered.

"Sweet!" Curtis slapped both their hands, then groaned when his cell phone beeped. He yanked it out of his pocket. "Third message from my dad. We'd better go."

Vivi started to get up, but Lane grabbed her hand. She was too high on life to let this moment pass just yet. "Wait! Don't you guys think we should, like, soak in the moment? We just found our Brandon!"

"Totally! A toast!" Vivi said, picking up her chocolate shake. "Here's to helping Isabelle be Sluttig-free. To Brandon!"

Lane lifted her soda glass, and Curtis grabbed one of the untouched ice waters. "To Brandon!"

★ ★ ★ ★ *ten* ★ ★ ★ ★

"What if he's never read any of the books that Brandon's supposed to like?" Lane asked as they walked back into Vivi's house later that night. "Or seen the movies? Oh my God. What if he doesn't watch *Extreme Makeover: Home Edition* like we said? Isabelle has every episode practically memorized! If he's never seen one, she's gonna know."

Vivi bit the inside of her cheek and tried not to snap. Lane was so putting a damper on Vivi's victory buzz.

"Okay, what happened to you between the diner and here?" Vivi asked. She whipped her suede jacket off and threw it toward the hooks next to the door. It missed by a mile and hit the floor, where she left it. "You were loving Jonathan half an hour ago."

"I know. And I still am. It's just . . . how are we going to turn a preppy boy with manners into a bad boy who plays the drums?" Lane paused on her way up the stairs. "Oh God! He's supposed to play the drums!"

"It doesn't matter!" Vivi said, frustrated. She charged ahead up the stairs and down the hallway. "They're just going to the prom! Do you think Isabelle's going to bring a drum set with her and demand that he play?"

Vivi pushed open the door to her bedroom and, as always seemed to be the case these days, there was Marshall, sitting at her computer. Over a plain burgundy T-shirt and those new jeans of his, he was wearing a trendy army green military-style jacket. It was the first time in her life Vivi had ever seen her brother sporting a totally unboring and semi-badass outfit.

"Nice jacket," Vivi said, tossing her bag on her bed. "Maybe you should, like, wear it outside the house where there are people. Instead of, you know, sitting in here where no one will ever see you."

"She's right, Marshall. You've been spending an unhealthy amount of time in front of the computer lately." Lane dropped onto the beanbag chair and forced all the air to wheeze out.

"I was bored and I happened to notice that Isabelle was online, so I just figured I'd chat," Marshall replied. He glanced at Vivi and tugged at his cuffs. "You really like it?"

"Yeah. It actually rocks," Vivi said offhandedly. She was too busy jumping three moves ahead in her mind. She leaned toward the computer, and Marshall quickly minimized the window he had been typing in. "You're on with Izzy right now?"

"Yeah. We were just talking about what we're doing this

summer and—" He paused, looking up at Vivi with sudden concern in his eyes. "Why do you look so happy?"

He glanced at Lane, who, Vivi noticed, looked rather green. What was wrong with her? They'd found a Brandon. And yet Lane looked more uncertain than ever.

"Why is she so happy?" Marshall repeated to Lane.

"We kind of found a guy," Lane explained, sounding like she was announcing an execution.

"Yeah, and she was all giddy about it half an hour ago before she started overthinking it, as always," Vivi groused.

Marshall's face was blank. "You found a guy."

"For Isabelle! To be Brandon," Vivi announced, refusing to let their negative vibe get to her. "IM her and tell her you want to take her to the prom."

"Wait a minute," Marshall said, standing up. He pushed the desk chair in with his butt, preventing Vivi from getting anywhere near her own computer. "You found a guy? Who is he?"

"His name is Jonathan Hess, and he is amazingly hot," Vivi explained, clasping her hands together as her heart fluttered at the very thought of him. "Isabelle is going to die when she sees him."

"How hot?" Marshall asked, gripping the top of the chair behind him.

"Why? Do *you* want to date him?" Vivi shot back.

"You know, after seventeen years, the gay jokes are getting tired, Viv," Marshall replied.

Vivi rolled her eyes. "Fine. I'm just saying. What do you care how hot he is? Just IM the girl." She reached past him, grabbed the mouse, and opened the window again. Marshall, just as quickly, reached over and closed it.

"No, Vivi. Hang on a sec," Marshall said, pushing his newly floppy bangs away from his head, where they flopped right back down. "I mean, where's this guy from? Are you sure he's not some deviant or something? Did you get references?"

"From who? His ex-girlfriends? God, Marshall, have a little faith," Vivi said. "Lane and I are not going to pick some guy out of a police lineup to take our best friend to the prom. He's a good guy. Now would you *please* just do your job?"

She reached for the chair and yanked it out, nearly knocking her brother over in the process. Marshall's shoulders slumped, but he sat down and pulled the keyboard tray toward him. His fingers were just about to touch the keys when Lane shoved herself up.

"Wait," Lane said, wringing her hands.

"What now?" Vivi asked, ready to burst from excitement and frustration. "This is no time to be squeamish. For all we know, she could be on the phone with Shawn right now telling him what color corsage will go with her dress. Which, by the way, he will totally ignore."

"I just want to be sure we're doing the right thing," Lane said, her forehead wrinkled with worry. "Are we totally positive we can change Mr. Prep into Brandon the Bad Boy? We only have two weeks, and he has to be totally believable."

Vivi wanted to scream. What did Lane think they were doing, brain surgery? All Jonathan needed was a little stubble, a leather jacket, and a fake tattoo, and they were in business. "Yes. We're totally sure," she said firmly. "Marshall, let's do this."

✳ ✳ ✳

"I left him a message last night, but he hasn't gotten back to me yet," Lane told Vivi. She paused outside her art classroom and sighed. "I hope he's not backing out."

Even though she did sort of hope that Jonathan was backing out. If he backed out now, it would definitely be too late to find someone else, and they could go ahead and bag the whole plan.

Lane took a deep breath and sighed. She had to remember why they were doing this. Isabelle was her best friend. All she was doing here was protecting her from Shawn.

"I knew I should have been the one to call him," Vivi grumbled.

"Why? What would you have said that would have been so different from what I said?" Lane asked, irritated.

"Nothing! I don't know," Vivi replied. She unzipped her yellow Nike hoodie and slipped it off to tie it around her waist. "It's just . . . I'm more forceful than you are, you know?" she said, yanking on the sleeves.

"Yeah. I'm aware." Lane looked around to make sure the coast was clear and lowered her voice. "That's why we decided I should call him. Since you're the one who almost scared him off."

"Whatever," Vivi said with a scoff.

Lane's fingers curled into fists, and she held her breath to keep from screaming. If Vivi wanted to do everything by herself so badly, why had she sucked Lane into this mess in the first place? It wasn't like she enjoyed scheming and lying and sneaking around.

"Hey, guys," Curtis said, coming up behind Lane.

Her heart stopped at the sound of his voice. But when she turned around to greet him, he looked morose. "What's wrong?"

"I'm out," Curtis said, shoving his hand into the pocket of his baggy jeans. "My dad found out I got a C on that Calc test, and he grounded me. No unapproved outings for the rest of the year. So I can't help you train Jonathan or whatever."

"You're kidding!" Vivi said, wilting visibly.

Lane's eyes stung unexpectedly, and she looked at the floor. She was already way too emotional to hear that Curtis was going to be MIA for this whole thing. Spending time with him was one of the arguments Vivi had used to talk her into the plan in the first place. And now she'd be spending *less* time with him.

"I'm really sorry," Curtis said, nudging Lane's elbow with his own.

Lane sucked it up and raised her eyes. "It's okay."

Then, behind Curtis, Lane saw Isabelle practically skipping toward them, a huge smile on her face. Lane's heart skipped an excited beat, even as her stomach turned. She had a feeling she knew what Isabelle was so happy about.

"Shhh. She's coming," Lane said.

Vivi's green eyes widened. "Hey, Iz!"

"You guys are never going to believe what happened!" Isabelle announced, jumping up and down in front of them. "Brandon talked to his parents, and they said he could come down for the prom! I'm going to prom with Brandon!"

"Oh my God, Izzy! That's awesome!" Vivi said, hugging Isabelle. "Congratulations."

She's good. I'd never know that she knew what was going on, Lane thought. Her heart pounded wildly, wondering if she could be half so convincing.

"Brandon? Who's Brandon?" Curtis asked, just as smoothly.

"He's this *incredible* guy Isabelle met on MySpace," Vivi said with a self-satisfied grin.

"Oh. Sweet, Iz," Curtis said.

"Yeah. That is *so* cool," Lane said calmly. She glanced at Vivi warily. "But do you really think that's a good idea? I mean, making a date with someone you met on the Internet?"

Vivi's eyes turned into tiny black dots. Lane knew that if the girl could have eviscerated her on the spot, she would have.

"What? I'm just worried about her," Lane said innocently. "What kind of friend just lets another friend go out with some random guy she met online? He might not even be a guy. He could be an old man. Or a woman! Or—"

"Okay, Lane, we get your point," Vivi said through her teeth.

Lane bit her tongue. She was only trying to say what she would have said if she had no clue that Brandon was actually Marshall.

"I knew you were going to say that!" Isabelle said, swatting Lane's arm. "And you're totally right. I already decided I'm going to e-mail him tonight and ask him to meet up somewhere this weekend so we can make sure we're both, you know, normal."

"This weekend? Really?" Vivi said, her voice tight. "That's so soon."

Lane gulped, knowing exactly what Vivi was thinking. If this pre-date went down the way Isabelle wanted it to, then they had only four days to get Jonathan up to believable Brandon standards. Four. Measly. Days.

At that moment, Lane's cell phone beeped. She whipped it out of her pocket and turned toward the wall. Technically students were not supposed to have their cell phones turned on during school hours, so she, her friends, and everyone else in school had become quite adept at hiding them from clear sight. She had one new text message, which she quickly opened and read.

Can meet 2day. My house. 4pm Call l8r & get detes. C u then.
—J

"Who is it?" Isabelle asked.

"Oh . . . uh . . . no one," Lane replied, quickly shielding the screen from her friends. "Just my mom saying she won't be home for dinner. Guess Dad and I are on our own again."

"Oh. Sorry, Lane. That sucks," Isabelle said, shuffling her books from one arm to the other.

Lane felt like she was going to burst into flames. Here Isabelle was commiserating for poor Lane and her subpar home life. Meanwhile Lane was lying to Izzy's face and plotting behind her back all at the same time.

"Yeah, well." Lane shrugged and quickly texted back.

OK. Thnx. Btw no shave 2day. Will xplain l8r
—L

She pocketed the phone and touched the sleeve of her sweater to her forehead, which was itchy with sweat.

"Everything okay?" Curtis asked pointedly.

"Fine. Dad and I are gonna go out. Around four?" she said, looking directly at Vivi. "Maybe someplace in Cranston?"

"Sounds like a plan!" Vivi said happily, winking at Lane for good measure.

Lane smiled, relieved that Vivi had so clearly gotten the message. Isabelle, meanwhile, looked at them like they were speaking in tongues. Which, in a way, they were.

"Um, isn't four kind of early for dinner?" Isabelle asked. "Doesn't your dad have to work?"

Lane's mind went completely blank. "He has the afternoon off, right?" Vivi said loudly, grabbing Lane's arm.

"Yeah. Didn't you mention that yesterday?" Curtis put in.

"What? Oh. Yeah. So we're gonna . . . go shopping first and then, you know, eat. Dinner. Together. After four."

Isabelle blinked. "Oh."

The bell rang. Ten seconds too late.

"See ya!" Lane blurted. She darted into class and grabbed the stool in the far back corner, hiding behind the easel that held her senior project. Her nerves didn't stop sizzling until the second bell rang and the door was closed. Thank God prom was less than two weeks away. This was not a lifestyle she could maintain for very long.

* * *

Lane was at her locker at the end of the day, rummaging through her things for her history notebook, when she felt someone watching her. She looked up to see Curtis's brown eyes hovering around the side of the locker door, and she yelped.

"God! You scared me," Lane said, blushing.

Curtis laughed and popped his gum as he came around the open door. "I've been there for, like, two minutes," he said. "You were deep in concentration."

"I can't find my history notebook, and we have an exam tomorrow," Lane said, tucking her red hair behind her ear as she crouched down to check the books on the floor of her locker. "I must have left it in class."

"You want me to go get it for you?" Curtis asked, pointing over his shoulder.

Lane's blush deepened at the chivalrous offer. "Really? Thanks."

"No problem. As long as you agree to go to the mall with me right now," Curtis said with a grin.

Right. Of course. He couldn't just be offering to something nice for her just to offer.

"I thought you were basically grounded," Lane sighed, hoisting her messenger bag onto her shoulder.

"Yeah, but even my dad knows a guy can't go to the prom without a tux," Curtis said.

Lane suddenly felt as if she were moving through mud. The prom. He was getting a tux for the prom. So that must mean he had a date. He had asked someone. And that someone had said yes. He wouldn't be dropping eighty bucks on a tux unless he was planning on using it.

"And you know I have, like, zero style, so . . . ," Curtis said, rubbing a hackey sack ball between his palms. Lane glanced at him. His ripped-in-seven-places jeans, the layered T-shirts, the watch she'd given him for his sixteenth birthday, which he wore every day. Had he been wearing it when he'd asked this random girl to the prom? The very idea made her ill. "What do you say? Will you come? I don't want to look like a tool."

For her. You don't want to look like a tool for her. Whoever she is, Lane thought.

"Hey, guys!" Vivi said, showing up at the exact perfect moment. Her cheeks were ruddy from eighth-period gym, and she was breathless from jogging all the way across the school. "Here. You left this in class," she said, slapping Lane's history notebook against Lane's chest. "Ready to go?"

"Yeah." Lane shoved the book in her bag and zipped it up. "We have plans, remember?" she said to Curtis. "Vivi and I are going to meet Jonathan."

"Oh, right," Curtis said, pushing his hands into his pockets. "Well, can't you, like, postpone it for an hour or something?"

"For what?" Vivi demanded.

119

"He wants to go to the mall," Lane explained.

"Uh, no," Vivi said, slamming Lane's locker for her. "This is Operation Skewer Sluttig, remember? This is way more important than shopping."

Curtis's eyebrows knitted. "But I—"

"You said you were out, and that's fine, but it doesn't mean you can bogart my main ally," Vivi said, slinging her arm over Lane's shoulders. "Besides, I thought you were grounded."

Then Vivi pulled Lane around a stunned Curtis and strolled off down the hall. "We'll call you and let you know how it goes!" Vivi shouted to him.

In her entire life, Lane had never been so grateful for Vivi's tendency to take charge and make decisions for her.

"You totally saved me back there," Lane said gratefully.

Vivi shrugged. "Don't I always?"

★ ★ ★ eleven ★ ★ ★

Waiting outside the front door of Jonathan's brick Tudor-style house, Vivi couldn't seem to make her knees stop bouncing. She held the box of books and movies Lane had put together in front of her, and the stuff inside kept knocking around.

"What's up with you?" Lane finally asked.

"Nothing. Just psyched to get started," Vivi replied, staring at the slats of the wooden door, the iron number *22* in the center. It was a big house, but not that big. And they'd rung the bell a good minute ago already.

"Yeah. Me too. Psyched," Lane said flatly. "But that doesn't explain why you're wearing that top. You're all . . . dressy."

Vivi's face reddened. Snagged. She had put on and taken off the trendy purple top her mother had bought for her birthday about ten times and eventually left it on. It had been hanging in her closet untouched for four months.

Not that she was trying to impress anyone, of course. Certainly not Jonathan. "It's not *that* dressy," Vivi said innocently, balancing the box of stuff on her hip.

"Yeah, but you're a T-shirt person," Lane said.

"And tank tops," Vivi pointed out.

"Yeah, but not—"

"Can we drop this, please?" Vivi snapped. "God, sometimes your whole 'I'm so observant' thing is a little annoying."

Lane's face crumbled, and Vivi instantly felt guilty. But just then the door opened and Jonathan stood before them in a worn gray Cranston Prep sweatshirt and distressed khaki shorts. He had somehow gotten even hotter overnight.

"Finally!" Vivi grumbled, striding by him.

"Come on in," he said wryly. "Sorry it took me so long. I was on the phone with work."

"You work?" Lane asked, stepping inside and looking around.

"Yeah. At the Cranston movie theater," Jonathan said, sticking close to Lane, Vivi noticed. "If you ever come by, I can get you free popcorn."

"Mmm . . . I *love* movie theater popcorn," Lane gushed.

"Are we doing this or what?" Vivi asked impatiently.

"Well, I can get *you* free popcorn, anyway," Jonathan said to Lane.

Vivi's face heated up. "You're hilarious, you know that?" she said, hovering near the foot of the wide staircase. She lifted the box slightly. "Where do you want this?"

"I guess up in my room," he said. "Second door on the right."

Vivi stomped up the wooden stairs and into Jonathan's room. It was a wide, airy space with a huge bay window overlooking the front yard, and it was neater than Vivi's room could ever hope to be. The sports photographs—a signed Derek Jeter, an old-school Ruth and Gehrig, a panorama of Yankee Stadium—were framed and spaced evenly apart from one another on the walls. The bed was made with plain blue sheets. The rattan throw rug was perfectly angled on the floor. The sweaters on the shelves in the open closet were folded, and the hanging clothes organized into sections of shirts, pants, and jackets. Even his shoes were lined up.

"Wow," Vivi said, marveling at the organization. "Anal much?"

"I just cleaned it," Jonathan said as he walked in.

"Oh, just for us?" Vivi tilted her head and let her long blond hair tumble over her shoulder.

Jonathan blushed slightly. "Do you guys, uh, want anything? Soda? Snacks? Anything?"

"You're such a good little host!" Vivi teased, sitting down on his bed. "But we're fine. Let's just get to work."

At that moment, Vivi's cell phone rang. Her heart all but stopped when she saw Isabelle's name on the caller ID.

"Crap. It's Izzy," she said, standing. "Where do I tell her I am?"

"I don't know," Lane said. "Make something up."

Vivi's mind was a complete void. "I can't say I'm at Lonnie's, because she might already be there. And I can't say I'm home, because she might want to stop by."

The phone trilled again.

"I can't take it! You answer it." Vivi tossed the phone at Lane.

"I can't! It's your phone, and I'm supposed to be out with my dad!" Lane threw the phone, and Jonathan picked it right out of the air.

"*If* she asks, just tell her you're out shopping. But only if she asks. The less detail, the better," he said calmly, handing the phone back to Vivi.

Vivi grabbed it, annoyed. If there was one thing she hated, it was when she lost her cool and someone else got to play the calm and collected one. But still, Jonathan was right. She swallowed hard and opened the phone. "Hey, Iz!" she said brightly.

"Oh my God, Vivi! Brandon is, seriously, *the* most amazing guy ever," Isabelle gushed.

Vivi's heart relaxed. "Really?" she said happily. "What happened?"

"He went on some florist's website and just sent me an attachment of five different corsages to choose from," Isabelle said. "He wants to make sure he gets it exactly right. Isn't that just the sweetest thing *ever*?"

"That's so sweet," Vivi said, flashing a thumbs-up at her cohorts. "This guy is going to be your perfect prom date."

"I know! Plus he said he'd be more than happy to come all the way down here this weekend so I don't have to drive," Isabelle added. "We're gonna meet at Lonnie's."

Vivi smiled. Marshall was doing his job so well. "That's great."

"I'm so happy I didn't call Shawn this weekend," Isabelle replied. "You guys totally saved me. And now all we have to do is get Curtis to ask Lane and find your perfect guy and we're good to go!"

Vivi glanced at Jonathan, who was watching her intently. "Yeah. Totally. We have to get on that," she babbled.

"Oops! I gotta go. He's IMing me right now," Isabelle said. "Talk to you later."

"Later!" Vivi snapped the phone closed. "She is totally in love with him."

"With who?" Jonathan sat down at his desk, pulled up his feet, and locked his elbows around his knees.

"With you!" Vivi said. "Well, Brandon. The guy we're going to make you into."

"Well, that's good, I guess," Jonathan said. "And see? She didn't even ask where you were."

"Yeah, yeah. You're very smart," Vivi said.

Jonathan grinned flirtatiously at her. "You know, I'm not the goody-goody you want to think I am."

Vivi smirked as he held her gaze. She had to concentrate to look away. "Okay. Are we going to do this, or what?"

"Yeah. What'd you bring me?" Jonathan asked Lane, peeking into the box.

"Just a bunch of stuff Brandon is supposed to like." Lane pulled a few books out of the box and handed them to him.

"Yeah. I checked out his page. He's into literature, huh?" He sifted through the novels, and then tossed them onto the bed near his pillow. "There's no way I can read all that."

Lane's jaw dropped. "You have to."

"I'm sorry. I'm a slow reader. Especially with novels.

Fiction is so annoying. You have to keep track of all these characters, you know? Remember how they look—"

"And who they know and what they like and where they're from," Vivi agreed. "I know exactly what you mean! I hate . . . imagining stuff."

"Wow. We finally agree on something," Jonathan said. He leaned back against his desk chair and crossed her arms over his chest. "If I'm gonna read something, I'd much rather read a historical book or a biography. Something that actually happened."

"Exactly!" Vivi cried.

"You guys," Lane said.

"If I could take two history classes and skip English entirely, I would totally do it," Vivi said.

"I know! And don't half the books they make you read just make no sense at all? Like *As I Lay Dying*. What the hell was that gibberish about?" Jonathan said.

"I *hated* that book!" Vivi agreed. "I actually threw it at my brother. He had a bruise on his arm for a week."

Jonathan looked at her quizzically. "Why at your brother?"

Vivi shrugged. "He kept telling me what a great piece of literature it was. He had to be stopped."

Jonathan laughed, and Vivi grinned. There it was again. That sexy laugh.

"You guys!" Lane shouted, standing up.

Vivi looked at her friend. For a second she'd actually forgotten where they were and why.

"We're kind of in a time crunch here," Lane said, ripping her jacket off. She looked at Jonathan. "I'm sorry if you hate fiction, but Isabelle loves to read. We hired you to do a job and part of that job is knowing these books. So you will read them."

She plucked *A Separate Peace* out of the box and handed it to him.

"And by the way, if you read history books and biographies, you still have to 'imagine stuff,'" she said, throwing in some air quotes. "It's not like you were actually there."

She sat down in a huff, and Vivi met Jonathan's gaze.

"Wow. I thought you were the tough one," he said.

"I've never seen her use air quotes before," Vivi replied. "You'd better take her seriously."

"Hello? I'm right here," Lane said, yanking out a printout of Brandon's MySpace page. "Now let's get to work."

✳ ✳ ✳

"This is a total disaster. We should just call it off. I'm serious. This is never going to work," Lane rambled as Vivi pulled up in front of her house. It was a cool evening, and she shivered in her jacket as a stiff breeze rustled the leaves of the oak in the center of her front lawn.

"Wow, you have a fabulously positive attitude," Vivi said, resting her hands on the steering wheel. "You should have been a cheerleader."

"I'm not kidding! He hasn't even read *Catcher in the Rye*!" Lane blurted. "Who hasn't read *Catcher in the Rye*?"

Vivi pulled a face and raised her hand. "Uh . . . me?"

Lane blinked. "Then how did you pass the paper?"

"It's this little thing called the Internet? Maybe you've heard of it. They have whole plots online," Vivi told her.

"Well, that's just great. Nice to know you're a cheater," Lane said, reaching for the door handle. She seriously felt as if she were going to explode. This had been a bad day even before Curtis and his tuxedo proposition, what with having to lie to Isabelle at every turn. But at Jonathan's house it had only gotten worse. Not only had he never read a single book on Brandon's list, he'd seen only a couple of the movies. Plus they had gone through his entire closet and hadn't found one thing that a guy like Brandon would ever wear, so now they had to spend the following afternoon walking Jonathan through the mall. And to top it all off, it was already past nine and Lane hadn't even begun to study for her history test tomorrow.

"You have to chill out," Vivi said, lowering her chin as she stared Lane in the eye. "You're taking this whole thing way too seriously."

"Yeah, well, somebody has to," Lane said. "If you could just take a step back from your evil hand-wringing for five seconds, you would see that this is never going to work."

"Evil hand-wringing?" Vivi said.

"Yeah! And by the way, in case you've forgotten, we have a history exam tomorrow. An exam which neither one of us had a chance to study for thanks to this project of yours," Lane said. "Unless you're just planning on cheating on that, too."

"Okay, first of all, enough with the personal attacks," Vivi said. Lane sat back, clenching her teeth in impatience.

"Secondly, we're seniors. You have a straight-A average. One bad test is not going to kill you. Besides, you could probably pull a C without even studying."

"I don't want to get a C," Lane said, throwing the door open. "And if I do, it's on you."

"Hey! Don't act like this is all my fault!" Vivi called after her. "We're doing this for Izzy, remember?"

Lane ignored her and speed-walked up to her house. Inside, she slammed the door behind her. This was *never* going to work.

★ ★ ★ twelve ★ ★ ★

"Remind me again why we need to shop," Jonathan said, following a couple of paces behind Lane and Vivi as they cut across the center of the Mall at Short Hills. He was looking around, head tipped back to take in the skylights, as if he'd never been in a mall before.

"Because Brandon is supposed to be a badass," Vivi said, quickly power walking. "And you are not."

"I told you. I can be a badass," Jonathan protested.

A toddler in a stroller dropped a rattle on the floor as her mother pushed her by, and Jonathan stopped to retrieve it, then jogged to catch up with them. He chatted with the mom for a couple of seconds, and Vivi couldn't help noticing how the sun pouring through the windows seemed to follow him. Ridiculous. When he returned, he was smiling over his good deed until he noticed Vivi and Lane staring him down and his face fell.

"What?"

"Oh, yeah. That was totally badass," Vivi said with a snort. "Come on. We have to get to work."

Vivi made a beeline for Hollister and headed straight for the back, where they kept the sale racks. She started pulling out distressed T-shirts and chose a couple of jackets off the wall. Immediately she recognized the army-green number her brother had been sporting the other day and grabbed it. If Marshall could make it look good, then Jonathan would make it hot.

When she turned around, Jonathan was standing in front of a mirror, wearing a pair of aviator sunglasses off the rack and checking himself out. Vivi's heart skipped a beat. This guy could model. Seriously.

"What's the matter?" Lane asked.

Vivi jumped. She hadn't noticed her friend standing at a rack of distressed button-down shirts just to her left. Lane glanced at Jonathan, then back at Vivi, as if she were trying to put two and two together and coming up with zero. Vivi crossed the crowded store and shoved the clothes at Jonathan.

"Here. Try these on."

Jonathan took off the sunglasses, and the very movement was sexy. Like he'd practiced doing it a thousand times, even though she knew he hadn't. And naturally, that made it even hotter. He grimaced at her armful of items.

"I would never wear this stuff," he said.

Vivi rolled her eyes. "That's kind of the point."

He shot her a sarcastic look, but took the clothes and

headed into the dressing room. Vivi casually leaned against the wall while he changed. When he folded his sweater over the top of the door, her breath quickened.

"So, are you really going to the prom stag?" Lane asked, inspecting a sweater with a faux-torn collar and frayed sleeves.

Vivi stood up straight. Could Jonathan hear them in there? And if so, what would he think of a girl who was going to her own senior prom without a date?

You don't care, she told herself. *It doesn't matter what he thinks, because he's Isabelle's date.*

"Yeah. No one worth going with, so why not?" Vivi said rather loudly.

Lane bit her lower lip and looked thoughtful for a moment. "Maybe I will, too."

"Really?" Vivi felt a dash of hope at the idea that she might not be the only one. On any given day, she could be as individualistic as she wanted to be, but prom night was a huge deal. It might be nice to have a wingman. Except— "Wait, Lane, I thought you were going to ask Curtis."

"Well, that was before he had a date," Lane said nonchalantly as she moseyed over to a sales rack filled with girls' clothes.

Vivi balked. "Curtis has a date?"

"Well, not definitely. He just—"

At that moment, the door to the dressing room opened and Vivi and Lane were cut short. Jonathan stood there, wearing the clothes Vivi had picked out for him, looking like a total tool.

"You didn't actually roll up your jacket sleeves," Vivi balked.

"What? It looked all messy," he replied. "And why would anyone buy a T-shirt that already had a hole in it?"

He held out the collar of the T-shirt—which was tucked into the waistband of his jeans—like it was covered in dog poo.

"You're such a dork," Vivi said, shaking her head at the sight of him.

A blush crept across Jonathan's face. "If I'm a dork because I don't understand this universal need to look like you just rolled out of bed, then I guess I'm hopeless," he said, rolling his eyes. "Hang on."

He closed the door, and the clothes he'd been wearing were once again flung over the top.

"Vivi? Uh . . . maybe you should try to not be so hyper-critical," Lane whispered. "He *is* doing us a favor."

"What did I say?" Vivi started to flip through the other shirts on the sales racks, just in case they had to go back to square one.

"You just called him a dork to his face," Lane pointed out, coming back over the men's racks.

"Oh, please. He's fine," Vivi said.

"Maybe. For now. But if you don't watch out, your critical side is going to scare him off, and then Izzy will be dateless," Lane hissed.

Vivi's heart squeezed. That was pretty much the last thing she wanted to have happen. And she didn't want to hurt Jonathan's feelings either. But had she already done it? Was he in there right now, wondering why the heck he'd agreed to this?

The door opened. Jonathan had changed into a gray T-shirt and short blue jacket.

Once again, he had rolled up his sleeves. He turned to the mirror, then to the side to check himself out.

"There. How's this?"

Lane groaned, folded her arms atop the clothing rack, and collapsed her head against them. Vivi sighed. This was going to be harder than she thought. You could take the kid out of prep school, but you couldn't take prep school out of the kid.

"Awful," she said, walking over to Jonathan. Time to take charge of the situation. She grabbed his arm and yanked the fold out of the sleeve, then did the same with the other. Then she knelt down and yanked down on the jeans so that they weren't sitting so high, and uncuffed the hems, leaving the fraying edges to cover the back of his shoes. When she stood up again, she yanked the T-shirt out of the waistband and reached for his hair.

"Whoa! What're you doing?" Jonathan asked, holding up a hand.

"Just trust me," Vivi said.

She shoved her hands into his hair and yanked up, then ruffled the back with her fingers. From the bench in the dressing room, she grabbed the aviator sunglasses and handed them to him. He paused for a second before putting them on. Together, Vivi and Jonathan faced the mirror.

Dear Lord, I am a miracle worker.

"Huh," Jonathan said, turning to the side. "That's not bad."

"Nope. Not bad at all," Lane said, joining them.

"So, this is the kind of guy your friend likes?" Jonathan asked, shuffling around to see himself from different angles.

"We're getting there," Vivi told him. "Now if you'd just let us do our job . . ."

Jonathan sighed and took the sunglasses off again. "All right, then," he said. "I give. You paid me. So you should make the decisions."

"So you'll read the books?" Lane asked hopefully, clasping her hands in front of her in excitement.

"As many as I can," Jonathan conceded.

"And you'll let us take you to the salon?" Vivi asked.

Jonathan checked his look in the mirror again and frowned in thought. When he turned back to Vivi again, his smile was heart-stopping.

He's Isabelle's date. Isabelle's *date,* Vivi told herself.

"I'm all yours."

Vivi's knees nearly buckled at the words. This was going to be trouble.

"Okay, so I'm going to skim *Catcher in the Rye* and *Farewell to Arms,*" Jonathan said, consulting the list he'd made at the food court. "Those are the two most important, right?"

"That should do it," Vivi said, the warm wind in her hair

as she drove Jonathan back home. "Now what are you wearing on your date this weekend?"

Jonathan smirked. "The T-shirt with the hole, the jacket with the frayed cuffs, the jeans with the fake dirt on them, and the black boots that look like they lived through World War Two."

"Good boy," Vivi said with a sly smile.

"Oh, and I can't forget the fake tattoo." He whipped out the black, twisted bicep cuff from the bag.

"Not that she'll see it, but it'll be good for your attitude," Vivi said. "It'll make you feel dangerous."

"I feel dangerous just looking at it," Jonathan joked.

"Don't forget to practice your monotone," Vivi reminded him. "And you'll want to keep the talking to a minimum. Cool guys answer with one syllable. Got it?"

"Cool," he said, lowering his voice.

Vivi laughed again. Date or not, she was having more fun than she'd had with the last three guys she'd gone out with combined.

"This guy your friend is in love with must be a real tool," he said, back to his normal voice. "I feel like I'm playing to the very worst in male stereotypical behavior."

"Yeah. That's Shawn for you," Vivi said darkly. "If I never see that jackass again, it'll be too soon."

"You know, when I first met you I thought you were just an insane control freak—"

"Wow. Blunt much?" Vivi said.

Jonathan laughed. "But now that I've spent some time with you," he continued. "It's pretty clear that you really are doing this to help out a friend. Which is cool. Slightly crazy, but cool."

Vivi blushed. She turned her head, pretending to check the next lane as she switched, so that he couldn't tell. Okay. This was very not good. Between the sweating palms, the pounding heart, and the easy blushing, there was no more denying that she had a crush on Jonathan. A guy she could definitely *not* have. Vivi was starting to wish she hadn't dropped Lane off on the way to Cranston. She wasn't sure she could trust herself alone with him. Vivi had never been big on self-control when there was something she wanted in her sights.

"So, you're going to your prom alone?" Jonathan asked. He took out the pair of sunglasses, which he'd bought for himself, and picked at the little UV protection sticker on one of the lenses.

Vivi cleared her throat. So he *had* overheard. How very humiliating. "Looks that way." She turned off at his exit and headed for his street, suddenly wanting more than anything to get him out of her car. The posh houses and lush lawns of Cranston zoomed by her without her so much as noticing them.

"Huh," Jonathan said.

Vivi turned on her blinker by whacking the control as hard as she could. "What?"

"Nothing," Jonathan said. He finally freed the sticker and shoved it into one of the bags at his feet. "I guess I'm just surprised you don't have a boyfriend."

Another blush. Vivi was starting to hate her skin. "Well, I did. We just broke up last week."

Jonathan slipped the sunglasses on and looked at her. "Oh? Why?"

Because he was a wuss bag who couldn't handle one small criticism. Well, one small criticism every hour or so. Like she was really going to tell Jonathan that.

"He was unworthy," she said with a sly smile.

Jonathan laughed. Damn that sexy laugh and the Hollywood eyewear.

She pulled up in front of his house and slid to a smooth stop. She was very impressed with her self-control. Slamming on the brakes would have been a much more satisfying move.

Jonathan removed the sunglasses and looked her right in the eye. "Yeah," he said. "I think most guys are probably unworthy of a girl like you."

Oh, God, kiss me, Vivi thought. *Kiss me, kiss me, kiss me.*

She found herself looking at his mouth, and noticed that tiny white scar on his chin again. "What's that from?" she asked.

"What? Do I have food on my face," he asked, quickly flipping down the visor mirror.

"No. The scar," Vivi said with a laugh.

"Oh, that?" Jonathan said. "I could tell you, but then I'd have to kill you."

"Ha ha. Seriously. How'd you get it?" Vivi asked.

"Doing something badass," Jonathan joked, his eyes teasing. He popped the car door open.

"Why won't you tell me?" Vivi demanded, not used to being shot down.

"Because it's more fun to make your face do that blotchy red thing it does when you're frustrated," he said, getting out and closing the door. "See ya!"

"Jonathan—"

"I've got a lot of work to do," he said, lifting his bags and waving. "Bye!"

"Fine!" Vivi shouted, half-laughing, half-annoyed.

"Fine!" he replied jovially.

Vivi shook her hand and peeled out, lifting her hand out the top of her car in a wave. She bit down hard on her bottom lip to stop herself from smiling.

"He's Izzy's guy. *Izzy's* guy," she said as she zoomed toward the highway. "Jonathan is all for *Izzy*."

thirteen

Lane glanced up from her English notes, yawned, and looked out the plate glass window at Lonnie's, where school buses and carpools were rolling by. It was so different here in the morning. Instead of the lively chatter of gossip, the place was relatively quiet, the peace disturbed only by the sound of the cash register pinging open or the occasional cell phone ring. Five men and one woman were in line, all wearing brown or black trench coats to ward off the slight drizzle outside. Lane glanced at her watch and wondered what train these people were catching. Her mother was out of the house by six every morning to get to breakfast meetings in the city by eight. Apparently the Lonnie-goers had less demanding jobs.

Outside on Washington, Vivi trudged by, the hood of her sweatshirt up over her head. At the same time, Isabelle approached from the other direction, walking jauntily, her pink plaid umbrella protecting her hair. They met at the door, and then Isabelle dragged Vivi inside and practically flung her into the booth across from Lane. Isabelle was all smiles. Vivi was giving off seriously irritated this-is-way-too-early vibes.

"Hey, guys!" Lane said brightly.

Vivi shoved her hood back and, with a grunt, accepted the coffee Lane pushed across the table to her.

"I am *so* sorry for the emergency meeting, but I have *the* biggest news!" Isabelle said, standing at the end of the table.

Lane looked at her quizzically. "What's up?"

"Shawn broke up with Tricia last night!" Isabelle announced, bouncing up and down on her toes.

Lane had never been punched in the stomach, but she had a feeling it would feel a lot like this. She actually lifted her two braids (a necessity for her frizzy hair in humid weather) and covered her eyes with them, not wanting to see Vivi's head actually explode.

"What!?" Vivi shouted, fully awake for the first time.

"He called me last night," Isabelle said. "Now, don't freak out. I did not get back together with him. And we didn't even talk about the prom."

"Thank *God*," Vivi said, slumping.

"But I do think he wants to go with me," Isabelle added.

"Iz! Come on!" Vivi blurted.

"But I was so good, you guys!" Isabelle said, ignoring Vivi's protestations. "I told him that he'd hurt me, and that if he wanted me back, he was going to have to earn it this time," Isabelle said, grinning like she'd just announced her biggest triumph ever.

"Wait, so you *are* getting back together with him?" Lane asked.

"What about Brandon?" Vivi added.

"Brandon will understand," Isabelle said, waving a hand. "You guys, this is Shawn. And it's our senior prom. And I'm sorry, but I think going with someone I know and love is a much better idea than going with someone I've never met."

Lane's heart beat an insane pitter-pat rhythm in her chest. This could not be happening. Isabelle could not really be considering getting back together with Shawn after everything he'd done to her—and after everything she, Vivi, and Curtis had done to try to protect her.

"But you're going to meet him! This weekend!" Vivi blurted, standing up.

"I can always cancel that," Isabelle explained. "Brandon won't mind not having to drive all the way down here."

"But . . . but . . . Isabelle! You like Brandon!" Lane said. "You can't just blow him off."

"She's right!" Vivi added. "Don't make any snap decisions."

Isabelle's face dropped slightly, and she looked at the freshly waxed floor, where her umbrella was making a small puddle. "You guys, I know you don't like Shawn—"

"This has nothing to do with Shawn," Lane lied. "We just . . ."

She looked at Vivi for help, widening her eyes.

"We just want you to keep your options open!" Vivi put her hands on the sides of Isabelle's arms and squeezed. "Iz, at least meet Brandon before you decide."

"Yeah. Just wait until after Saturday," Lane added, turning on the bench so that her legs were dangling over the edge. "Then you'll be able to make an informed decision."

"We saw how Brandon made you feel," Vivi implored. "And that was just on IM. Imagine what it would be like to hang out with him in person! Iz, he might be, like, your soul mate!"

Lane almost laughed, but bit her tongue. She knew how much effort it must have taken Vivi to utter the phrase "soul mate" without rolling her eyes.

"You think?" Isabelle said, raising her eyebrows.

"Totally!" Lane put in, feeling like a complete heel. But there was nothing else she could do. Jonathan was their only hope. "But, if you blow him off now, you'll never know."

Isabelle sighed, her shoulders slumping. She stared down at her manicured fingers and fiddled with the cord on her umbrella. "Maybe . . ."

"Come on. It's just one date. One meeting," Vivi said.

"And if you still want to go with Shawn after that, we'll shut up about it," Lane added. Vivi glared at her, but Lane shrugged. Honestly, if Isabelle picked Shawn after meeting Jonathan, there really *was* nothing else they could do for her.

"Okay. Fine," Isabelle said with a resolute nod. "I will not get back together with Shawn without giving Brandon a shot first."

"Yes!" Vivi cheered loudly.

"Good decision," Lane said.

"Thanks, you guys." Isabelle gave Vivi a quick hug, then leaned down to cheek-kiss Lane. "Sometimes you two are good to have around," she joked. "Want anything? I'm gonna grab a bagel and juice."

"I'm good," Lane said.

"Me too," Vivi added, finally sitting down again. She waited until Isabelle until was on line with the trench coat patrol and out of earshot before speaking again. "Whew. That was close."

"Tell me about it," Lane said, pulling her notebook closer to her. "But now we have to make sure that Jonathan is seriously irresistible. Shawn is going down!" Lane whispered, her eyes sparkling.

"Wow. You're really into this all of a sudden," Vivi said, amused.

"Well, that was scary!" Lane hissed, glancing across the shop at Izzy, who was inching forward on the line. "I do not want her getting back together with Shawn. And obviously Brandon is our best chance."

"Hm. Haven't I been telling you that from the beginning?" Vivi said nonchalantly.

"Yeah, yeah," Lane said. "So you were right. Don't let it go to your head."

They looked at each other and smirked. "Too late!" they said in unison.

Then Lane laughed and settled back to study. First she was going to ace her English quiz and then, this afternoon when she and Vivi met up with Jonathan, she was going to throw herself into this project for real. After this close call, *nothing* was more important than keeping Isabelle away from Shawn.

✷ ✷ ✷

Lane was hanging out in front of the school after the final bell, waiting for Vivi as the younger kids ran for the busses and the older kids headed for their cars. She tipped her head back slightly as the sun attempted to peek its way through the clouds, and she smiled. Her English quiz had been a snap. In face, she had finished twenty minutes before the end of the period and spent the rest of the time coming up with quizzes to test Jonathan's knowledge of the various books she'd given him. He had to have read at least a couple of them by now, and if not, Lane was going to sniff him out.

It was Taskmaster Morris from here on out.

"Getting a tan?"

Lane's head snapped forward, and she opened her eyes to find Curtis standing before her, one foot on his skateboard. Her face turned crimson. "Oh . . . I was just . . . uh . . ."

"What are you doing now?" Curtis asked, popping his skateboard up and into his hands.

Lane swallowed hard. "Vivi and I are going to Jonathan's."

"Oh." He looked off toward the parking lot, put the board back down, and pushed it back and forth with his toe. "I was gonna see if you wanted to do the Calc homework together."

The sun pushed its way farther through the clouds, and Lane's skin prickled with heat. "I'm sorry. I can't," she said, wishing more than anything that she could. "This morning

Isabelle told us she's getting back together with Shawn unless Brandon is, like, her soul mate. So we kind of have to—"

"Make him into her soul mate?" Curtis supplied.

"Yeah." It sounded stupid now that someone else had said it out loud.

"Okay. I guess I'll go, then," Curtis said, hopping on his board. He hadn't looked her in the eye in two minutes.

"Wait!" Lane blurted. "Are you mad?"

"No. Operation Skewer Sluttig is important," Curtis said flatly, shrugging and looking pointedly toward the parking lot. "You gotta do what you gotta do. Catch you later."

And then, he zoomed off down the hill, lifting a hand in a wave, but not looking back. Lane's stomach was all tied in knots. Curtis had never been that cool to her before. Not in all the years that she'd known him. Did he have a problem with Jonathan? With the plan? What had she done to offend him?

"Hey, Lane!" Vivi shouted, jogging up behind her.

Lane shook off her negative vibe and turned to her friend. Time to put her game face on. She could obsess about Curtis later.

"Hey! You ready to go?" Lane asked, trying to reclaim the determination and excitement she'd been feeling moments ago.

Vivi yanked her backpack straps onto her shoulders. "That's what I came over to tell you. You can have the afternoon off," she said.

Lane blinked. "What?"

"You can have the afternoon off," Vivi repeated, slapping

her shoulder. "Kick back. Relax. Or, you know, study. Since that's what you always want to do anyway," she joked.

She started past Lane, who stood there dumbly for a good five seconds before finding her voice.

"What are you, my boss?" she asked.

Vivi stopped and turned to her, looking surprised. "No. It's just that Jonathan's gonna watch some of the movies we gave him, so our services aren't needed," she said. "Well, yours aren't, anyway. I said I'd go over there and watch them with him."

Lane studied her friend. Vivi checked her watch and suddenly became very interested with the long line of cars jockeying for position at the parking lot exit. The longer Lane stared at her cheek, the pinker that cheek grew.

"What?" Vivi snapped finally.

"Oh my God. You like him!" Lane blurted. "That's why you don't want me to go! You want him all to yourself."

Vivi huffed, but still looked out at the traffic. "You're cracked."

"I so am not!" Lane blurted.

Vivi stood up straight and stared Lane right in the eye. "I do not like him. I only offered to go over there because I'm not entirely sure he's going to get the appeal of *Dead Poets Society*."

"But you don't get the appeal of *Dead Poets Society*," Lane reminded her.

"Well, no, but Isabelle explained it to me once, so I can just regurgitate that to him," Vivi replied. "It's just business," she added, looking away again. She could barely stifle a giddy smile.

"Oh, God! It is so not! You like him! I don't care what you say. You like our best friend's fake boyfriend!" Lane had to will herself to keep from screeching.

"Lane, please—"

"Vivi, you can't do this. If you go over there alone, you could screw up the whole plan," Lane begged, throwing her arms out at her sides. "You . . . Jonathan . . . alone in the dark. Watching semi-romantic movies . . . I know you. You'll jump him. You won't be able to stop yourself!"

"Do you really think I have no self-control?" Vivi snapped.

"No! But—"

But when you want something, you usually go for it without thinking about other people's feelings. Lane couldn't say that to her. Vivi would flip out.

"Okay. I know you like to think that you know me and Isabelle *so* well, but this is one time that you have no idea what you're talking about," Vivi said. "I am not about to jeopardize the whole plan and send Izzy running back to Shawn, just because I may be *slightly* attracted to Jonathan. Every girl he knows is probably attracted to him."

Lane glared at Vivi. "I'm coming with you." She pushed past Vivi toward the parking lot, but Vivi put out her arm, stopping her.

"No. You're not," she said, holding Lane back.

"Vivi!" Lane cried.

"Lane!" Vivi replied, crossing her arms over her chest.

For a long moment, Lane engaged in a staring contest with Vivi, feeling like she was back in kindergarten fighting over the last cupcake. She was not going to back down. Not after blowing off Curtis—who was now apparently mad at her—so that she could go to Jonathan's. She was as much a part of this plan as Vivi was. There was no way she was going to be shut out now. But the longer they stood there, the more Lane felt herself cave. There was no winning with Vivi. There never had been. There never would be.

"Fine. If you want to obliterate this whole thing, be my guest," Lane said finally. "I don't care anymore."

She turned on her heel and stormed off the other way, headed for home. For the first time in Lane's life, a pack of freshmen jumped out of *her* way. Apparently she looked intimidating when she was about to burst into tears.

"I'm not going to obliterate anything!" Vivi called after her.

"We'll see!" Lane shouted back, sure that Vivi couldn't hear her over the roar of an approaching bus.

We'll just see.

☆ ★ *fourteen* ★ ☆

Vivi couldn't move. If she did, her shoulder would brush Jonathan's. Or their hands would touch. Or their thighs. What the heck was up with this tiny love seat thing? Jonathan's parents obviously had money. They couldn't afford bigger furniture?

"Can't we watch this in the living room? There's no air in here," Vivi said, looking around the actually quite airy family room.

"DVD player in there is broken," Jonathan said without tearing his eyes off the screen.

Perfect. Whoever had put together that faulty piece-of-crap technology was going to ruin her entire plan. Because if she moved just one inch, if she took an extra deep breath, some part of her body was going to touch some part of Jonathan's, and then it would all be over. She would attack him. She wouldn't be able to stop herself.

"This is actually pretty good," Jonathan said.

Vivi turned her head to look at his profile. It was perfect. He was perfect. And they were sitting on this loveseat all alone while his brother was at a friend's. No parents, no nosy brothers . . .

Wait. You do not like him. He's just a hot guy, Vivi told herself. *There are hot guys everywhere. You wouldn't even be* thinking *about kissing him if Lane hadn't put the idea in your head.*

Yes. This was Lane's fault. All Lane's fault. And she could prove the girl wrong. She *would* prove her wrong. All she had to do was keep her hands and lips to herself.

"What?" he asked, turning to face her.

She ripped her eyes away, refocusing on the TV. Her heart pounded so hard, it was making her nauseated. "Nothing."

He was still watching her. Staring at her cheek. Vivi rubbed her hands together and shoved them like a wedge between her tightly crossed thighs, trying to make herself as small as humanly possible.

Suddenly, Jonathan's thigh grazed hers. Her heart completely stopped. She looked at him, and he was somehow much closer than he'd been a moment before. His eyes were heavy as he took her in, the question in them perfectly clear. The plea for permission. Every inch of Vivi's body throbbed.

Yes. Do it. Just kiss me.

Jonathan's lips swooped toward hers, and much to her own surprise, Vivi leaned away.

"Stop!"

"What? What's the matter?" Jonathan sprang back as if burned. Vivi was already on her feet.

"Nothing. It's just ..." Behind her, Robin Williams was going on and on. "It's just this is Isabelle's favorite part of *Dead Poet's Society*. You should watch it. You have to . . . to know it if you're going to go out with her on Saturday."

Jonathan glanced at the TV screen as if it were an alien ship that had just landed in his family room. He sat up straight on the velvety love seat and pressed his hands into the cushion.

"Right. I actually wanted to talk to you about that," he said.

"About what?" Vivi asked.

"About me dating your friend." Jonathan stood up, not taking his eyes off Vivi's face. He stood so close to her, she could feel his warm breath on her face. God, he was perfect. Why did he have to be so perfect? "Vivi, do you . . . really want me to date your friend?"

Vivi thought of Isabelle's tears when Shawn cheated on her. Her confidence after she met Brandon online. Her excitement after Brandon had asked her to the prom. The deal they had made that Isabelle would give Brandon a chance.

Vivi was standing in front of the only person who could prevent Isabelle from going back to Shawn. Izzy had been her friend since they were both in pigtails and pink overalls. Jonathan had been in her life for three days.

"Yes. I do," she said firmly. "Why wouldn't I?"

"No reason," he said, his face turning to stone. "I guess we should go back a couple of scenes."

He grabbed the remote and sat down at the far end of

the love seat, pressing his side against the arm, giving her as much room as possible. Vivi felt tears prickling behind her eyes.

"Actually, I have to go," she said loudly, grabbing her bag.

"What? We're not even done with the first movie yet," Jonathan said.

"I know. I just remembered I have to do something."

She was not going to cry in front of him. No way. No how.

"But, Vivi—"

"I'll see you later!" Vivi was already halfway through the kitchen. "Just watch as many of those as you can!" she shouted back.

She slammed the front door behind her and sprinted for her car. It was for her own good, for Isabelle's. For everyone's sake.

★ ★ ★ *fifteen* ★ ★ ★

Friday was gorgeous and sunny, and the courtyard in front
of the school was jam-packed with students chatting and
popping their skateboards, soaking up every last minute
until they had to go inside for homeroom. Lane leaned back
against the outer wall of the gym, waiting for Vivi to arrive
so they could update one another on their progress. She kept
one eye on the parking lot and one on Curtis and his skater
friends, who were among the boarders, trying to impress a
group of freshmen girls with their skills. Curtis hadn't spoken to her all morning, which meant her stomach was already
clenched beyond repair, but it got worse every time one of
the girls laughed or giggled. Was one of them Curtis's date?
When Vivi's convertible finally pulled in, Lane jogged over to
meet her friend at her designated parking space, happy for
the reprieve from the low-rent X Games.

"Okay. What happened between you and Jonathan last

night?" Lane demanded before Vivi even had a chance to get out of her car.

"God! Give a girl a heart attack, why don't you?" Vivi demanded.

Vivi was wearing low-slung sweats and her track T-shirt, her hair in a ponytail with no makeup. Standard Vivi don't-mess-with-me gear. Lane knew it. She *knew* something had gone wrong with Jonathan.

"Did you guys hook up? Is that why he was acting so freaky on the phone last night?" Lane stepped back so Vivi could open her car door.

"You talked to him?" Vivi demanded. "What did he say?"

"Oh my God, I'm right! You kissed him, didn't you?" Lane demanded.

"No, all right? We did not hook up!" Vivi slammed her car door. "Why were you guys talking on the phone?"

"He called me to go over the IM conversations between Marshall and Isabelle," Lane told her. She watched her friend closely, gauging her reaction to every word. "He wanted to make sure he was ready."

"Okay. So why the big panic?" Vivi asked.

"Because, he was acting weird. Very businesslike. No jokes, no nothing. And he asked me if I'd talked to you since you left there," Lane continued as they turned and headed back toward the school. "Why did he ask me that?"

"Lane, I have no idea. I'm not a mind-reader, all right?" Vivi said with a shrug. "All we did was watch a movie. No big deal."

"If you say so," Lane replied.

"I say so. How did it go with the IMs?" Vivi asked, pulling her sunglasses out of her bag and sliding them on. "Are we all set?"

"Not exactly," Lane told her. "I mean, there were a *lot.* Have Marshall's grades been suffering lately? Because I honestly don't think he's been doing anything other than chatting with Izzy."

Vivi snorted. "Figures. It's the first time in his life a girl's spoken to him past the 'hey' stage," she joked.

"That's not true! I talk to him," Lane protested. They had arrived at the circle of benches in the courtyard and sat down on the only one that was still free.

"Yeah. Because you have to," Vivi replied.

"I don't understand what your problem is with your brother," Lane said, dropping her bag down at her feet.

Vivi rolled her eyes and tipped her head back with a yawn. "Whatever. Is Jonathan ready or not?"

"There's no way he's going to remember everything," Lane replied. "It's too much. I mean, he's a smart guy, but this is like cramming for finals in two days. Anyone would have a hard time. And if Izzy asks him one weird question on something he doesn't remember, we're dead. What're we gonna do?"

Vivi pulled her head up and stared out across the parking lot in a forlorn way that gave Lane an even deeper twist in her stomach. She looked almost resigned.

And then Vivi's entire face lit up. "I've got it!"

"What?" Lane asked, both hopeful and nervous at the same time.

"There you are! I've been looking all over for you guys!" Isabelle trilled suddenly, coming up behind them.

Vivi's face went ashen and Lane jumped in to distract Izzy before she could notice.

"Hey, Iz!" she said, grabbing her friend into a hug. "So! Tomorrow's the big date! Are you excited?"

"So excited," Isabelle said. "I can't wait to find out what he looks li—"

"Actually," Vivi interrupted suddenly, standing up. "Lane and I were just talking about tomorrow, and we think we should come with you."

"What?" Isabelle asked.

"Yeah, what?" Lane echoed.

"You know, what we were just talking about?" Vivi said pointedly, knocking Lane with her arm. "It's just, you met this guy online and he doesn't even have a picture up. He could be some, like, fifty-year-old perv or something. Or a kidnapper. He could be anyone."

Lane stared at Vivi. This was her solution to the problem? To go on a three-way date with Jonathan? What were they going to do, pass him notes under the table to tell him what to say?

"Well, we're meeting in a public place," Isabelle countered, shading her eyes from the morning sun.

"Yeah, but that's not enough." Vivi crossed her arms over her chest. "You've seen *Without a Trace*. Trust me. You want someone with you."

Isabelle bit her lip and looked at her friends. "You really think he's a fifty-year-old perv?"

"No! Of course not," Lane said, grasping Isabelle's hand quickly. "I'm sure he's a total gentleman. But Viv's right. It's better to be safe."

"You're right," Isabelle said finally. "And you guys should meet him anyway. We're all going to be hanging out together at prom!"

"Yes, we are," Vivi said through a forced smile.

Lane glanced at Vivi. Could it be any more obvious that *she* wanted to go to the prom with Jonathan?

"You guys are the best, have I told you that?" Isabelle reached out to hug them both. "What would I do without you?"

You'd be going to the prom with a jerk, Lane thought, her heart clenching painfully. Lane shielded her eyes and looked out over the school courtyard, bustling with kids reluctant to go inside on such a beautiful day. To her left, Curtis flew by on his board, jumping from an entire set of stairs on the pathway. *But at least you'd be going with the person you wanted to go with in the first place. Unlike the rest of us.*

There were couples everywhere. Lane wasn't sure if it was spring fever or the impending prom or just a random twist of evil fate, but everyone seemed to be holding hands, smooching in the halls, and flirting shamelessly everywhere she went. Standing in the cafeteria line behind Cara Johnson and Sanjay Medha was like watching a Skinamax production live and in full color. In front of the pair was a huge open space. Behind them was a long, long line. But all they could see was the extreme close-up of each other's noses as they nearly swallowed each other whole.

"Say something," the sophomore girl behind Lane urged under her breath.

Lane turned purple. She was no good at speaking up, but as the next person in line and the only senior in sight, she supposed it *was* her responsibility.

"Uh, excuse me?" she said meekly. "We kind of, um, need to get moving."

She was greeted with a loud, slobbery, sucking noise as they readjusted their faces. The kids behind Lane groaned. And then, like an angel descending from heaven, Curtis appeared, cutting the line to get in front of Lane. Her heart felt like it was going to explode at the very nearness of him.

"Yo! Gupta! If we wanted to see that, we'd rent the professional version!"

Sanjay and Cara pulled apart and looked over the line in a bored way, but they did move. They slid their one tray along, each holding one end, their legs practically entwined as they tripped forward. The kids in line cheered.

"Thanks," Lane said tentatively.

Curtis grabbed a chocolate milk and an apple. "Yeah, well, it was the least I could do."

"What do you mean?" Lane asked. She slid her tray behind his, taking nothing. Somehow food was the last thing on her mind.

"Just that I owed you one," Curtis said, glancing at her

from the corner of his eye. "I'm sorry about yesterday. I think I was a BFJ."

Lane laughed. She was so relieved, she could have kept on laughing for an hour. "You weren't a big fat jerk."

"Okay. Maybe a little fat jerk." Curtis joked. He took out his wallet and glanced at Lane's tray. She realized nothing was on it and quickly grabbed a bagel and juice. "I got both," he said to the lunch lady.

Lane was beaming as she emerged from the line. She and Curtis walked slowly side by side down the center aisle.

"I'm just irritated by this whole grounding thing. And you guys are so busy with Brandon. . . . I just feel like I'm never gonna get to see you unless we're studying together." He stepped sideways so he could look at her.

Lane's heart went kinetic on her. He was worried about never seeing her. This was the best conversation she'd ever had.

"Want me to call your dad and tell him he's evil?" Lane asked, trying to stay calm.

"Like you'd ever really do that," Curtis joked back, pausing in the center of the aisle. "Besides, he's not totally evil. We made a deal that if I get a B-plus or higher on that history test, I can go to this one party this weekend. So I have to wait till we get it back in seventh to find out if I can actually go, but I was thinking . . . if I can go . . . maybe you'd want to go too," Curtis said. "I'll pick you up, I'll drive you home. You don't have to do a thing."

"Really?" Lane squeaked. Was this a date? Were she and Curtis going on a date? "I mean, yeah, sure. That sounds good."

"Good!" Curtis said with a grin. "I'll pick you up around seven. Cool?"

I'll pick you up around seven. It sounded like a date. But no. She and Curtis were just friends. The guy quite possibly had a date for the prom. She had to calm down. Maybe his prom date was going to be there, too. Maybe he'd invite Vivi and Isabelle as well. *Do not let yourself get carried away,* Lane told herself.

"Okay. Cool," Lane agreed with a nod.

"Hey, are you guys gonna sit down, or are we eating lunch here?" Vivi said, coming up behind them.

Lane flinched, but managed not to drop anything. Together, the three of them headed off to join Isabelle at their table. Lane sat down, trying to invest herself in the talk about graduation and the post-graduation party, but she just kept waiting for Curtis to bring up this weekend's bash—to invite Vivi and Isabelle—but he didn't. He didn't so much as mention it.

Looked like it was just her and Curtis. Oh, and maybe his prom date. But Lane would deal with that if and when it happened. For now, she was just going to be happy. Happy and, for once, hopeful.

★ ★ ★ *sixteen* ★ ★ ★

Vivi's leg bounced up and down under the table in the back corner of Lonnie's. She pressed her hands down on her thigh to try to get it to stop, but it was no good. She was nervous. Like she was going out on a first date. Which, she supposed, she was. Only it wasn't her first date, it was Isabelle's. Isabelle's first date with Jonathan.

And of course, Isabelle looked like a goddess. Smooth hair, perfectly understated makeup, and a lovely, girly outfit that would have looked like a Halloween costume on Vivi. Isabelle had even refused to order anything to eat, not wanting to mess up her lip gloss. Vivi, meanwhile, had already polished off half a bagel with peanut butter and a bag of Doritos.

"Are you sure this dress isn't too much?" Isabelle asked, smoothing the front of her cotton Ralph Lauren strapless.

"Well," Vivi started to say. "Maybe—"

"No, Iz," Lane said, shooting Vivi a silencing look. "You look beautiful."

Isabelle smiled. "Thanks for coming, guys. What would I do without you?"

Vivi grinned, but Lane looked so uncertain it gave Vivi a sour feeling in her gut. But no. No. They were doing the right thing. They were keeping Isabelle away from the toxic substance that was Shawn Littig and handing her the most amazing guy on the planet. They were, quite possibly, the best friends ever.

Isabelle checked her delicate silver watch. "Where is he? You don't think he's ditching, do you?"

If he does, I will personally hunt him down and burn all his preppy little sweaters. "No," Vivi said, glancing at the neon clock on the wall. "He's still only fashionably late."

Just then, the glass door swung open. Vivi turned around, her heart in her throat. But it wasn't Jonathan who walked through the door of the restaurant. It was Marshall and his frizzy-haired, *Lord of the Rings*–obsessed friend, Theo. Vivi rolled her eyes and clucked her tongue as she slumped down again.

"Hey, Marshall!" Lane called out, waving.

Marshall looked up and smiled. "Hey, Lane." He said a few words to Theo, then came over as Theo got on line behind a pack of junior girls from the cheerleading squad. Marshall was wearing that new green jacket of his over a black T-shirt and yet another pair of trendy jeans. He even wore a studded black belt. His blond hair was uncharacteristically mussed.

"What are you doing here?" Vivi demanded, annoyed.

"Can't a guy get lunch?" he asked smoothly. "Hey, Isabelle."

"Hey," Izzy said. She glanced at him quickly, but then did a double take. "You look different."

"Thanks," Marshall asked, smiling shyly. "I think."

"Can I talk to you for a second?" Vivi asked through clenched teeth. Without waiting for an answer, she grabbed his arm and dragged him toward the counter. "What are you doing here? She's gonna know something's up!"

"Uh, Vivi? This place is always filled with people from school. Theo and I are just getting lunch. People do it all the time," Marshall said. "And besides, I wanna see this guy. I'm as much a part of this plan as you are."

Vivi glared at him. She actually couldn't argue with that. "Fine. But get your food to go. As soon as he gets here, you're out."

"Whatever," Marshall said, rolling his eyes.

Vivi balked as he turned around and strolled over to the counter. Apparently the new, tough wardrobe was going to his head. He said something to Theo, and they both chuckled, glancing over at Isabelle and Lane. Vivi could have killed him. What better way to ruin the vibe of a date than to have creepy genius boy spying on them? She stormed back to the table and dropped onto the bench. All she wanted was to get this song and dance over with already.

"Omigod. That's him. Is that him?" Isabelle said suddenly. She positively glowed.

Lane's face went totally slack. "That's him. I mean . . . it's gotta be," she added quickly.

Vivi whipped around, and the world stopped spinning. Jonathan stood at the door, slowly surveying the room. He slipped his sunglasses off, and his eyes finally fell on her. Vivi felt as if the heat emanating from her body could have warmed the rest of the shop. He looked incredible. His blond hair was perfectly disheveled, and he'd grown out a bit of blond stubble all along his cheekbones and chin—but not over his scar, she noticed. It was a hot day, so he had deviated from the agreed-upon wardrobe, but he'd done well. He wore a red T-shirt with black block writing over one shoulder and a pair of baggy, torn jeans. His black boots were scuffed, and he was wearing—unfortunately—the exact same belt as Marshall. Not that anyone other than Vivi would ever notice.

"Brandon?" Isabelle asked.

Slowly, Jonathan smiled. An intensely sexy, closed-mouthed smile. He strolled over to the table, his eyes never leaving Vivi's face.

"Hey," he said, looking deep into Vivi's eyes.

Vivi replied in a near whisper. "Hey."

"Hi," Isabelle added.

Vivi's shin exploded with pain—thanks to a kick from Lane—and she snapped out of it. She kicked Jonathan's foot, and he finally focused on Isabelle. Vivi watched with a mixture of dismay and triumph as his smile widened.

"Isabelle?" he asked, pleasantly surprised.

"Brandon," she replied, grinning wildly.

"Your photo did you no justice," Jonathan said, his voice low and husky.

Isabelle blushed with pleasure. "Thanks."

He reached into the back pocket of his jeans and produced a perfect pink rose. Isabelle gasped. "Pink's your favorite, right?" Jonathan said.

"You remembered," Isabelle said breathlessly.

Jonathan shrugged. "My grandfather always told me, never show up for a date empty-handed."

Vivi had to concentrate to keep from shaking her head at his brilliance. He'd been told how much Isabelle loved and respected her grandparents. This guy was good.

"That's so sweet," Isabelle trilled, sniffing her flower.

Jonathan sat down next to Vivi, across from Isabelle, and Vivi scooted away a touch, just to be safe. After Izzy introduced "Brandon" to her two friends, Vivi and Lane were finally able to exchange a look without being obvious. Lane beamed with pleasure, and Vivi smiled back. Her heart squeezed painfully, but she ignored it. It didn't matter what stupid reactions her body chose to have. Because Isabelle was obviously happy. And that was all that mattered.

"I have trouble sleeping sometimes. Too many thoughts, you know?" Jonathan said, narrowing his eyes in a smoldering way. "Like last night was really bad. I didn't get to sleep until about four in the morning."

He was slouched back in his chair, legs spread, toying with the straw in his soda. The complete antithesis of his usual, straight-backed, polite self. Vivi was amazed. He was doing it. He was really doing it. Isabelle was riveted. Vivi, mean-while, was wondering how much of what Jonathan was say-ing was true, and how much was stuff he made up for his Brandon character. Because the more he talked, the more she and Jonathan seemed to have in common. If this stuff was, in fact, true.

"I have the same problem," Vivi couldn't help mention-ing. "Like I just can't turn off my brain."

"Do you?" Jonathan asked, for a split second falling back into his real voice. That was how Vivi knew that this part, at least, was true. Then he seemed to recall himself and slipped back into character. "Anyway, so when that happens I usually play my guitar for a little while to relax."

Vivi's heart thumped, and she glanced at Lane, who went white as a sheet.

"Guitar? I thought you played drums," Isabelle said, con-fused.

There was the briefest, almost indiscernible twitch in Jon-athan's expression, but Vivi was pretty sure she was the only one who caught it.

"Yeah, but it's kinda hard to play drums in the middle of the night," he said, sitting up and leaning in toward Izzy. "I do still live with my parents. Unfortunately."

Isabelle grinned. *Good save,* Vivi thought.

"But when the guitar doesn't work, I have all these lists I recite in my head," he continued. "That usually does the trick."

"Lists? What kind of lists?" Vivi asked.

"Oh, you know. The states and capitals. The presidents,"

Jonathan said, then glanced at Isabelle. "Boring crap like that," he added. "Usually puts me right out."

"Omigod! I totally do the same thing! Except I try to recite the names of all the people in our class," Vivi said.

"Really? That seems like a lot," Jonathan replied.

"It's a small class," Lane said flatly. She kicked Vivi's shin under the table again.

Jonathan glanced at Lane, cleared his throat, and then returned to Isabelle. "What do you do when you can't sleep?"

"Me?" Isabelle blushed. "Oh, well, I don't usually have that problem. Ever. I usually pass out as soon as my head hits the pillow."

"Oh." Jonathan looked disappointed for a moment, but then smiled a completely sexy smile. "Well, I envy you. And your pillow."

Isabelle giggled and blushed even deeper. Vivi rolled her eyes. She almost couldn't believe how easily her superintelligent friend was falling for this ruse. Not that she minded. She was feeling quite proud of herself, actually. When her heart wasn't panging in that annoying way.

"So . . . are you sure you don't mind coming all the way down here again next weekend?" Isabelle asked.

Vivi held her breath. Was this it? Had Isabelle made up her mind to go to the prom with Jonathan? And if so, why did Vivi suddenly feel like screaming instead of jumping up and down for joy?

"For you? Are you kidding? I'd drive to California," Jonathan said without missing a beat. He leaned his elbows on the table, hooked his finger around Isabelle's pinkie, and held it there. Vivi couldn't have ripped her eyes off those entwined fingers if the Starbucks across the street had spontaneously combusted.

Isabelle smiled and held his gaze. "Good answer."

Jonathan smiled back. Vivi could practically feel the attraction between them. She was actually growing hotter from her proximity to it.

"Does that mean I passed the test, then?" Jonathan asked, cocking his head to the side and smiling that sexy, intimate smile again.

Isabelle blushed. "This wasn't a test."

"Sure it was," Jonathan said. "But I was more than happy to take it."

Isabelle turned her hand, lifted Jonathan's, and laced their fingers together. There was no moisture left in Vivi's throat.

"Then yes. You passed the test," Isabelle said, never taking her eyes off his.

Jonathan squeezed Izzy's fingers, and he may as well have been squeezing Vivi's heart. *Please let this be over soon,* she thought.

"Good. Then I'll be here next week," Jonathan said. "Just name the time and place."

"We're meeting at my house," Vivi blurted.

Jonathan looked at her like he'd forgotten she was there—or that she existed at all—and dropped Isabelle's hand.

"Cool. Well, you'll e-mail me the details, right, Isabelle?" he asked, drawing himself up in his seat. "I should probably hit the road. I've got a . . . thing. Back home."

Isabelle jumped to her feet. "Okay. I'll walk out with you."

"Cool." Jonathan looked at Lane, and then held Vivi's gaze for a long moment. "Ladies."

"Nice to meet you," Lane said loudly.

"Bye," Vivi added.

As they walked out the door together, Isabelle turned around with a gleeful grin and mouthed the words *"Oh my God!"* like she just could not take how lucky she was. Vivi forced herself to smile back.

"Wow." Vivi swallowed hard and kept the smile on. "How perfect was he?" she said to Lane.

"Yeah. Perfect," Lane said in a strained voice. She pushed herself up and out of the booth. "For you."

"What do you mean?" Vivi asked, scooting to the edge of the vinyl booth. "Isabelle's freaking."

"Yeah, because she's blinded by his gorgeousness," Lane said, throwing up a hand. "But I swear, Viv, it was more like he was on a date with you than her. You guys talked practically the entire time!"

"Give me a break, Lane. They were drooling all over each other at the end there," Vivi stood as well, her adrenaline shoving away her melancholy. "I'm happy for her!"

I am. I really, really am.

"Yeah. Sure. You just keep telling yourself that," Lane replied.

I am! I really, really am!

At that moment, Isabelle burst back through the door and skipped over to Vivi. "Omigod. I cannot believe how perfect he is! I'm so glad you guys didn't let me get back together with Shawn. I had *no* idea there were even guys like him out there. And he was so nice to you guys! Could you even imagine Shawn chatting with you like Brandon did? That would never have happened."

"Nope. Never," Vivi said, smiling triumphantly at Lane.

"This is going to be the best prom ever!" Isabelle said, showing every one of her perfect teeth. "Okay. Now I have to pee. I've had to for, like, twenty minutes, but I didn't want to get up from the table."

She laughed as she ran past her friends for the bathroom at the back of the shop. Ever so slowly, Vivi turned to Lane, eyebrows raised. But Lane simply scowled, refusing to board the happy train.

"Great. Now she's totally in love with him," Lane said, putting her hands on her hips. "What's she going to do when she finds out that Brandon is not really Brandon?"

"Okay, do you even know what a bright side is?" Vivi snapped as Lane headed past her for the door.

"Not in this scenario!" Lane turned around again, her arms crossed over her chest. "She's going to get her heart broken all over again!"

Vivi looked around the now semi-deserted, post-lunch-rush shop, grasping for an answer that would actually appease Letdown Lane. "Well, then . . . we just won't let her find out."

"Uh-huh. And how's that going to work?" Lane asked, leaning one hand on the back of an empty booth.

Vivi drew a blank and raised her palms. "I guess I'll just have to figure something out."

"Yeah, well, good luck with that," Lane told her. "Because either they date forever with Jonathan calling himself Brandon, or he's going to have to break up with her without breaking her heart. Try pulling that off."

Lane turned and stalked toward the door again, all in a huff. Vivi jogged over to get in front of her, blocking the exit.

"What's the matter with you?" Vivi demanded. "You don't get to take the high road all of a sudden and act like this is my fault. You're just as much a part of this as I am."

Lane sighed, staring at the floor. "Yeah. Maybe you're right. But I really wish that I wasn't," she said, looking sad. "I'll talk to you tomorrow."

"Wait! Where're you going?" Vivi stepped in front of her again. "We're supposed to meet up with Jonathan."

"You go. You don't need me there, anyway," Lane replied morosely.

This time, Vivi just let her go, and Lane shoved the door open with the heel of her hand, so hard it seemed like the thing would snap off its hinges. Then she was gone. And the second she was gone, everything she'd said sank right in.

Vivi felt the sourness of guilt seeping in around her heart. All she had wanted to do was show Izzy that there were cool guys out there who were not Shawn Littig, but instead, Isabelle was clearly crushing hard on *one* guy—on "Brandon." Vivi was going to have to figure out a way out of this that wouldn't involve Isabelle's heart breaking.

✳ ✳ ✳

After dropping Isabelle off at her house, Vivi drove straight to the Suburban Diner, where she, Lane, and Jonathan had had their first meeting. Her heart was pounding as she turned into the parking lot, but she told herself she was just excited to go over the next phase of the plan. It had nothing to do with seeing Jonathan alone. Her palms were not, in fact, sweating.

She expected to meet him inside at a booth, but as she tooled through the lot looking for a space, she saw him leaning back against the rear of his beat-up SUV. He'd smoothed his hair down again, but was still wearing the Brandon gear. Vivi grinned and waved, then pulled in alongside him and got out of the car.

"You were amazing!" she shouted, rushing around the car. Jonathan stood up straight as she approached. "Really. Unbelievable. I had no idea what a good actor you were. Isabelle bought it like you were giving it away on sale."

"Yeah. She seems like a cool girl," Jonathan said.

"I am so excited you are going to the prom with her," Vivi rambled. "Shawn Littig is finally, *finally* history!"

"Vivi . . . about the prom," Jonathan said, pushing his hands into the pockets of his jeans. "I don't think I can go."

Vivi felt like she'd just stepped in a tremendous pothole. "What?" she blurted. "You have to go. She's so excited! And you just told her you'd be there! You can't back out now!"

"Vivi." Jonathan took a step toward her, his blue eyes searching hers. "I don't want to go unless it's with you."

Vivi's heart spasmed. "What?"

"There's something here. Between you and me," he said. "Not between me and Isabelle. You're the one I want, Vivi."

Then he placed his hand on the small of her back and pulled her to him. Before she could suck in a breath, his lips touched hers. Vivi felt an explosion of attraction unlike anything she'd ever felt before. She sank into Jonathan, and his tongue parted her lips, sending shivers all down her back. Then her arms were around his neck. His thighs were pressed against hers. His hands were in her hair. There were no thoughts in Vivi's mind. Nothing at all other than how incredibly perfect this felt.

And then, a horn honked.

Startled, Vivi pulled away. "What the hell are you doing?" she shouted, half out of it.

A car full of teenage boys rolled by them, laughing and taunting them. Vivi wiped the back of her hand across her mouth as if she was disgusted, even though she was anything but. He had to believe that she was, though. He had to. Because she could not go there. Jonathan was Isabelle's date. He was meant for Isabelle.

"You're supposed to be dating my best friend!" Vivi said firmly, taking another step back to put more space in between them.

"No, *Brandon* is supposed to be dating your best friend!" he shot back, his face red. "*I* want to date *you*!"

Vivi's breath was short and shallow. This was not happening. It simply was not happening.

"Vivi. Come on," Jonathan said quietly, stepping toward her again. "Go out with me. We both know we want this," he said with an adorable smirk.

One look at Jonathan's hopeful face, and she knew. She'd screwed up. Big-time. It wasn't just Isabelle who was going to get her heart broken around here. All thanks to her and her stupid plan.

"No. I don't," she said flatly.

Jonathan took a step back and laughed in an awkward way. "What?"

"I don't want to date you, Jonathan. You are so not my type, you may as well be another species," Vivi said, the words coming as if of their own accord.

"You don't mean that," Jonathan said, his face turning bright red.

"Yes. I do. Look at you. You're like a nineteen-fifties movie. The uptight, preppy, fresh-faced jock with the little brother he just loves and the dorky clothes and the . . . the whole 'I'm so polite' thing. That's not me. None of that is me," Vivi said. "I'm messy. I'm loud. I don't do polite. You and me? We don't mesh."

"What about opposites attract?" Jonathan asked beseechingly as he reached for her hand.

Vivi groaned and snatched her arm away. Jonathan flinched. "God! Can you not take a hint!?" she shouted, exasperated. "We are not going to be together! I don't like you that way!"

Jonathan's jaw clenched and he stared at her, betrayed. He looked like Vivi had just run over his dog.

"I'm sorry," Vivi said automatically, her heart twisting. "That was . . . blunt."

"Yeah, but you don't do polite, right?" Jonathan snapped, backing away from her.

"No, it's just. I wanted to be clear," Vivi said, grasping at straws. "If you're going to the prom with Isabelle—"

"No. I'm not. I'm not going to the prom with Isabelle. This ends right here," Jonathan said, turning toward his truck.

"Jonathan, no," Vivi said desperately. "Stop."

Jonathan got in behind the wheel and slammed the door so hard that Vivi lost her breath. She couldn't let him go. She couldn't let him drive away and risk never seeing him again.

"I'm sorry, all right!" she shouted over the revving engine. "Come on! Let me explain!"

But he ignored her. He simply pulled out of the space and drove away, not even giving her one last glance.

✴ ✶ seventeen ✶ ✴

"Come on, come on, pick up!" Vivi said through her teeth. She was clutching the steering wheel with one hand and her phone with the other. Normally she was all about cell phone safety, but this was an emergency situation, and her headset had gone MIA. Probably crushed under one of the empty fast food bags or piles of gym clothes that polluted her car. "Pick up!"

"Hi. You've reached Jonathan. Leave a message."

"Dammit!"

Vivi threw her phone on the passenger seat, where it bounced and came dangerously close to flying out the window. She ran a yellow light, made a sharp left, and careened down Washington Street.

This was a nightmare. How could Jonathan do this to her? If he liked her so much, shouldn't he be trying to help? Shouldn't he not be backing out on her at such a crucial moment? Didn't he get it by now? This was not about her. It was not about the two of them. It was about Isabelle.

Her cell phone rang and her heart leapt. She nearly drove into a fire hydrant groping for it. When she finally grasped it in her sweaty fingers, it was almost on the fourth ring and she didn't even have time to check the caller ID. This call could not go to voice mail.

"Hello?" she said shrilly.

"Vivi? Are you okay?" Isabelle asked.

"Oh. Hey, Iz. I'm fine," Vivi said, stopping at a red light and cursing to herself for not making it.

"You sure? You sound a little weird," Isabelle said.

"No. I'm good. What's up?"

"I just can't stop thinking about Brandon," Isabelle gushed. "Did you notice that little scar on his chin? Where his stubble wasn't growing in? How insanely sexy was that?"

"Insanely," Vivi agreed morosely.

"What do you think it's from? Do you think he got it recently, like, skiing or something? Or do you think it's one of those old scars, like from a block battle in kindergarten or something?" Isabelle theorized.

Vivi took a deep breath. She was not going to lose it. She was not. But why did Isabelle have to be so darn romantic and dramatic and mushy? It was going to kill her when she found out Jonathan—Brandon—whoever—had backed out.

Maybe I should just tell her now. Get it over with, like ripping off a Band-Aid.

"I wonder if he'll tell me," Isabelle continued rapturously.

"Or maybe it's, like, some deep, dark secret thing from his past and I'll have to wheedle it out of him."

Vivi hit the gas when the light turned green and zoomed toward Lane's house. *Okay, we have to fix this. We cannot give up now,* she told herself. *Jonathan will go to the prom with Isabelle if it kills me.*

"Vivi? Are you there?" Isabelle asked.

"Iz, I'm sorry, but I kind of have to go. I'm driving," Vivi said, appealing to Isabelle's goody-goody nature.

"Oh! Sorry! Call me later, okay?" Isabelle asked.

"I definitely will. Bye!" Vivi dropped the phone again, slammed on the brakes in front of Lane's house, and ran up the front walk. She pounded on the door to let out some of her psychotic adrenaline. After what seemed like forever, Lane yanked open the door, her face creased with concern.

"Vivi! What's the matter with you?" she asked.

"Jonathan bailed," Vivi said, sweeping past her friend into her large foyer.

"What?" Lane gasped. Her face went white and she let the front door slam shut.

"He bailed!" Vivi grabbed the banister on the wide stairs and squeezed. She was so pent up, she felt like she could break the solid oak in half. "He said he's not going to the prom."

"What? Why?" Lane asked.

All right. This one was going to hurt. "Because he . . ." Vivi took a deep breath. "He likes me. He wants to go with me."

Lane looked suddenly faint. She leaned back against the wall next to the door and stared. "I knew it."

"Yeah, yeah, you were right. Congratu-freakin-lations,"

Vivi said, pacing in front of her friend. "He likes me and I like him. But that should not change the fact that we had a deal!"

"Forget the deal!" Lane blurted, covering her face with her hands. "We have to call it off. It is beyond time to call it off."

"No! We can't! Not now!" Vivi said, her fingers splayed before her like a condemned man begging for his life. "Not now that she's met him! Not a week before the damn prom! It's too late. If she doesn't go with Brandon, she doesn't go with anyone. And this is Isabelle! She's Suzy High School! If she doesn't go to her prom and win prom queen and all that she'll . . . she'll kill herself!"

Dramatic, Vivi knew, but even Lane couldn't deny it. Isabelle had been looking forward to their senior prom ever since ninth grade. She had made a collage for a health class assignment—a work that was supposed to represent the person she wanted to be—and every picture had been cut out of a prom magazine. She still had the damn thing stuck inside the inside flap of that stupid Prom Planner of hers.

"So call him," Lane said tiredly. "Call him and make him change his mind."

"You don't think I tried that? He won't pick up the phone," Vivi said. She collapsed onto the bottom step of the staircase. "You know, sometimes I think caller ID was the worst invention ever."

"Yeah, only when you're on the calling end," Lane replied.

Vivi sighed. It was go time. Time to tug on the last straw. "Lane, you're gonna have to go over there and talk to him."

"Me?" Lane looked like a cornered street dog.

"Yes, you! I know I screwed up, and I'd fix it if I could, but I can't. You're the only one that can fix it," Vivi begged. "Please. He won't listen to me, but maybe he'll listen to you." She glanced at her watch. "It's still early. You can catch him before dinner."

"You want me to do this *now*?" Lane asked.

"Yes, now," Vivi said. "We're already losing precious time. Besides, if we don't fix this, I'm going to be up all night worrying about it."

"Well, I'm sorry to hear that, but I can't," Lane said resolutely, shaking her head. "I can't go over there. I have plans."

For the first time, Vivi noticed that Lane's hair was pulled prettily back from her face and her eyes were all made up. And not only that, she was wearing a cute cotton dress Vivi had never seen before. She looked nice. But what could she possibly be doing that would be more important than saving Isabelle from a dateless prom?

"Please, Lane? We can't let this fall apart now. We've come too far," Vivi said. "You're the one who was all worried about Isabelle's broken heart. What do you think's gonna happen if we have to write her an e-mail from Brandon saying he can't come after all? She'll think he met her and didn't like her. She'll think he thought she was hideous or something. Talk about a broken heart—she'll be shattered."

Lane stared at Vivi, venom in her eyes. "You did this, Vivi. I warned you this was going to happen, but you didn't listen. It's not my responsibility to clean up your mess."

Vivi felt a brand-new thump of guilt in her chest. Technically, Lane was right. This was all Vivi's fault. But that didn't change the fact that it needed to be fixed. For Isabelle's sake.

"Please?" Vivi whispered. "Come on, Lane. For Isabelle. Please?"

Lane took a deep breath and stared off down the hallway to the kitchen. For a split second, Vivi was sure that she'd failed—that all hope was lost. But then, Lane looked at her again, her expression resigned and her shoulders slumped.

"Fine," she said, lifting a weak hand and letting it drop. "I just have to make a call."

* * *

Lane pulled her mother's Jaguar to a stop in front of Jonathan's house and killed the engine. She speed-dialed Curtis for the third time and held her breath. As the phone rang, she checked out Jonathan's house, half-hoping to find the driveway empty and the house all closed up. Unfortunately several windows were open to let in the warm spring air, and she could hear music coming from an upstairs window. Finally the phone clicked over.

"Curtis here. Today's song is 'Graduate' by Third Eye Blind."

Lane groaned through the few bars of the song she'd already heard two times in the past half hour. Finally, mercifully, the beep.

"Curtis, it's Lane again. Did you get my other messages?" she asked as she climbed out of the car and slammed the door. "I'm so sorry I had to run out, but if you call me and give me directions to the party, I'll meet you there. So, just . . . call me. Okay. Thanks. Bye."

She hung up and shoved the phone into her jacket pocket. Why hadn't Curtis called her back yet? Had he not gotten her messages? Was he at her empty house right now ringing the doorbell over and over again? Or had he gotten the messages and was just so mad, he didn't even want to call her back?

I hate Vivi. I hate, hate, hate, hate, hate her! Lane thought as she speed-walked to the front door and rang the bell.

Feeling murderous by this point, Lane rang the bell again, pushing it so hard, she was pretty sure she sprained her finger. She was still shaking out her hand when Jonathan opened the door. His face registered obvious surprise.

"Hey," Lane said, suddenly realizing she'd been so busy trying to call Curtis that she hadn't remotely planned out what to say.

"Hey," he replied. "Come in."

He ducked his head and shoved his hand in the pocket of his madras shorts. Maybe it was a good thing Vivi hadn't come herself, because in his baby blue polo, with his tan legs exposed, looking all sheepish, he was totally adorable.

Jonathan led Lane into the kitchen, where his mother—a tall preppy woman with short blond hair—was chopping vegetables.

"Mom, this is my friend Lane," Jonathan said. "Lane, my mom."

"Hi," Lane said, feeling awkward.

Jonathan's mother wiped her hands on her apron and

smiled. "Hi, Lane. Nice to meet you." Then she looked at Jonathan quizzically.

"We're just gonna go in the family room for a sec, okay?" Jonathan asked.

"Sure. Do you want anything to drink or eat, Lane?" she asked.

"No thanks," Lane said.

"Well, call me if you need anything," she said, before returning to her chopping.

Jonathan turned and walked down a couple of steps into the family room. Playing on the TV was an episode of *Junk Brothers*, one of "Brandon's" favorite shows. Lane raised her eyebrows at Jonathan.

"Yeah. You guys got me into this," he said, lifting the remote to mute it. He walked around the coffee table and stood, facing her. "So. What's up?"

"Nothing. Sorry if I'm bothering you," she said.

"You're not. But my friends are gonna be here in a minute," he said. "So . . ."

"So why am I here?" Lane asked.

"I think I know why you're here," Jonathan replied, scratching the back of his neck and looking away, like he was embarrassed. "Vivi told you what happened."

"She told me you quit," Lane said. "So I was just hoping to talk you back into it."

"Wow. And you sound very enthusiastic about it," Jonathan joked.

Lane managed a weak smile. She walked around and perched on the arm of the velvet love seat. "Look, I know you think we're both insane, but Isabelle's not. She's actually incredibly cool and sweet and awesome. And she's the one that's gonna be hurt if you don't come. Maybe we shouldn't have started this whole thing, but we did. So I guess I'm just asking you to consider her feelings."

Jonathan looked at her, almost amused, and Lane realized what she was saying. She chuckled and looked at the floor, feeling like a complete idiot.

"Consider the feelings of a total stranger who you are in no way responsible for," she said, nodding her head.

"I'm sorry," Jonathan said. "I really am. But I knew from the beginning I shouldn't have gotten involved in this. I know you think what you're doing for your friend is a good thing, but it's not. You took away her chance to make a decision for herself."

Lane's heart felt hollow. Jonathan had no idea how ironic his words sounded to her. She felt as if she'd never made her own decision for herself ever in her life, and now he was accusing her of making Izzy's decisions for her. Was that what she had done? Was it possible that, by participating in Vivi's insane scheme, she was taking more charge of Isabelle's life than she'd ever taken of her own?

She realized at that moment that she had known this was never going to work—that she had no chance of talking Jonathan in to coming back. After all, she wasn't the type-A personality of her particular group. But she'd come anyway. She'd come because it was somehow easier than looking at Vivi and saying no.

Jonathan picked up his backpack from the floor and yanked a thick envelope out of the outside pocket.

"Here," he said, handing it to her. "It's the money Vivi paid me. I appreciate your situation, Lane, I really do. But it's your problem. Not mine."

"Okay," Lane said, her voice thick with tears. She couldn't believe this was happening. Isabelle was going to be crushed, and it was all her fault. Hers and Vivi's. Not only was Izzy going to be dumped by the person she had called her "dream guy," she was also going to have no date for the prom. Unless Shawn hadn't asked someone yet, and then she'd be going with the devil himself. How had it all gone so wrong?

"You all right?" Jonathan asked. "You look like you just lost your best friend."

"Or all three of them," Lane said morosely. Vivi was going to be pissed. Curtis was going to be hurt. And once Isabelle got dumped, she was going to sink into the biggest depression of her life. All because of one stupid little scheme.

"What do you mean?" Jonathan sat on the opposite arm of the love seat and put his feet up on the cushions.

"You don't want to hear about it," Lane said, blushing.

"Wouldn't have asked if I didn't," Jonathan said with a kind smile.

Lane glanced at him. Could she really tell him what was wrong? She'd gone so long without really telling anyone what she was really feeling. But why not Jonathan? He was a nice guy, and it wasn't like he was going to tell anyone what she said. He'd basically just cut all ties with her and her friends. Lane shoved his money into her purse and turned to him.

"Do you remember Curtis?" she asked.

"The guy from the diner the first night. Sure," Jonathan said. "He's been IMing with my brother about video games."

Lane smiled. "He has?"

"Danny thinks he's way cooler than I am," Jonathan said with a laugh. "Why?"

"The thing is, I've liked him basically forever," Lane said, shoving herself up and pacing toward the bookcase on the wall. "And he . . ."

"He has no idea," Jonathan finished for her.

"Kind of," Lane said.

"Why haven't you said anything?" Jonathan asked.

"Because I can't!" Lane said, feeling pathetic. "I've planned it out, like, a million different ways, but every time I try I chicken out. And every time I chicken out I feel like an even bigger loser. Plus, he's been my friend, like, forever. And if things go wrong, I don't want to lose that."

"Ah."

"But then the other day he asked me to go to this party tonight and, I don't know, maybe I'm just reading into it or whatever, but I think he was asking *me*, you know? Like as his date?" Lane said hopefully.

"This party is tonight?" Jonathan asked, pointing at the floor.

"Yeah."

"Then why the heck are you here?" Jonathan asked.

Lane's face turned purple. She toyed with the spine of an old book on one of the shelves. "Because Vivi made me come."

"She *made* you?" Jonathan blurted.

"Well, yeah! I mean, we had to save the plan, right? And she couldn't come over here so—"

"Lane, don't take this the wrong way, but get out of my house," Jonathan said, not unkindly.

"What?" she gasped.

Jonathan walked around the coffee table and put his hands on her shoulders. "Do you realize what's going on here? You've wanted this guy your *entire* life and tonight might have been your best shot with him, but instead you're here, doing what you think will make Vivi happy. What you think will make Isabelle happy. What about you?"

Lane's heart started to pound. He was right. He was totally right.

"Vivi has totally messed with your mind," Jonathan continued, bringing his hands to his temples in frustration as he paced away. "She's somehow got you believing that her plan to help Isabelle is more important than anything. Even more important than you or me. Well, that's crap!"

"You're right!" Lane replied, her adrenaline pumping. "That *is* crap!"

"You're important! You're a beautiful, smart, funny girl! I think you should track this Curtis dude down and tell him he'd be an idiot not to go out with you," Jonathan ranted, throwing his arm out.

"Yeah! He would!" Lane grabbed her purse.

"Good! Now go!" Jonathan said with a smile, pointing at the door.

"Okay! I will!" Lane replied, all riled up. She turned and stormed up the stairs, but stopped at the door and turned her head. "You really think I'm beautiful, smart, and funny?" she asked quietly.

"Go!" Jonathan said with a laugh.

And she did, as quickly as possible, grinning the whole way.

"Everything okay, Lane?" Mrs. Hess called after her.

"Everything's fine! Nice to meet you!" Lane shouted back.

Then she slammed the front door of Jonathan's house and ran for her car, her heart pounding with excitement.

It has to work. It has *to,* Vivi thought, clutching her cell phone as she walked upstairs to her room after a big bowl of ice cream. *Please, Lane. Pull off a miracle.*

She was just shoving through the door to her room, where Marshall was sitting—as always these days—in front of the computer, when her phone rang. Vivi's heart slammed into her rib cage. Lane.

"Lane! What happened?" Vivi blurted into the phone.

Marshall turned around in the desk chair and leaned forward, elbows on his knees. Vivi had already apprised him of the situation, so he was all ears.

"He didn't go for it," Lane said, sounding strangely giddy. "He's out."

"What?" Vivi blurted. The room started to spin. Marshall hung his head in his hands.

"He's out," Lane repeated. "Sorry. I gotta go."

"Sorry? *Sorry!?*" Vivi blurted, gripping the phone so hard, her fingertips hurt. "Lane, where are you? You can't just give up! We've got to—"

But the line went dead. Vivi groaned and speed-dialed Lane right back, but it went directly to voice mail.

"Dammit!" Vivi blurted, tossing her phone on her bed.

"He didn't change his mind?" Marshall asked.

"No, Marshall, he didn't change his mind," Vivi replied sarcastically, crossing her arms over her chest. "Oh my God. What are we going to do? There has to be something we can do," she said, starting to pace.

Marshall stood up and walked to the window, staring out on their quiet street. "I hate to say this, Vivi, but I don't think there is," he said quietly, chewing on his thumbnail.

"Marshall," Vivi blurted, frustrated. "If you say 'I told you so,' I will hurl you right out that window."

"I'm not!" Marshall replied. "But what are you going to do? Hire a stand-in? It's too late! She's met the guy now. If he's not coming to the prom, then no one is."

Vivi's heart had never felt so sick. She moaned and sat down on the edge of her bed, putting her elbows on her thighs and her head in her hands. "This is not happening. It is not happening. . . ."

Isabelle was going to be devastated. Crushed. And why? All because Vivi had concocted this stupid plan. "I thought I was doing the right thing," Vivi said, looking up at Marshall, her feet bouncing up and down. "I didn't want her to let Shawn hurt her again. No one did."

"I know," Marshall said simply. "And there was a point there when I really thought it was going to work."

"Really?" Vivi said, tears springing to her eyes.

"Really. But unfortunately . . ." Marshall looked over at the computer screen. Vivi stared at its whitish-blue glow.

"It didn't," she said, her voice flat. Her heart was so heavy, it was making her shoulders curl forward. This was it. This was the end. She felt as if she'd just resigned herself to a life of friendlessness and solitude. "You need to write to Isabelle and tell her Brandon can't come to the prom."

"You're sure?" Marshall said.

"What else can we do?" Vivi stood up and letting her arms drop at her sides. "The sooner we do it, the better. We can't leave her waiting until prom night thinking she still has a date."

Marshall took a deep breath and laced his fingers together on top of his head, his elbows jutting out like wings. Then he blew out the breath and turned toward the desk, determined. "Okay. Let's do this."

He brought up Isabelle's MySpace page with her smiling face up in the lefthand corner. Just looking at it made Vivi want to smack her head against the wall. She couldn't be here for this. She had to go.

"I'll be downstairs," she told Marshall, grabbing a pillow off her bed.

"Wait a minute. You don't want to tell me what to write?" Marshall asked.

Vivi paused at the door. She felt the tears threatening. Like she had any idea how to let a person down easy. Like she could even remotely bring herself to do this to her friend. She looked at her brother, so wide-eyed and innocent, and her heart panged. "You're way nicer than I am, Marsh," she said. "I'm sure whatever you come up with will be fine."

Vivi jogged down the stairs to the first floor, suddenly needing to put as much distance as possible between herself and the mess she'd created. Her eyes stung from unshed tears and her throat felt tight. She'd failed. She'd failed her friend in the worst possible way. Just thinking about how Isabelle's face would look when she read Marshall's e-mail made her want to hurl something. And it was all her fault. She raced for the basement and its comforting, cool darkness. It wasn't until the door closed behind her that she finally let the tears flow.

✶ ✶ eighteen ✶ ✶

After driving around the entire town of Westmont twice, searching for Curtis's mystery party and finding nothing but a policeman's retirement bash at the VFW Hall, Lane sat on her front step and waited. Her parents were out at some big gala in the city and wouldn't be home until the wee hours of the morning. Which was good. Because at least she knew Curtis would get home before them and they wouldn't find her passed out in front of the door. At least she hoped he would get home first. If he stayed out all night, she was pretty sure her adrenaline rush would be gone by the next time she saw him.

Finally, a pair of headlights flashed around the corner. Jeff's Mustang. Lane stood up, her heart leaping into her throat. She wiped her sweaty palms against the back of her jeans and waited for Jeff to pull into Curtis's driveway. Waited for Curtis to get out and knock fists with the two guys in the backseat. Waited until he turned around and finally saw her.

"Lane?" he said.

Somewhere off in the distance, thunder rumbled. Wind tossed Lane's hair across her face. She shivered and pulled her jacket closer to her as she walked across her lawn to meet him in his driveway. He was wearing a blue sweater with frayed cuffs and a pair of cargo shorts, and his hair was all styled into a perfect mess. He was adorable.

"Hi," she said. "Did you get my messages?"

He lifted his hand to show her that he was holding his phone. "Just now," he said, his tone apologetic. "I didn't even realize I had my phone off."

"You just got them?" Lane asked, relieved.

"Yeah. When I came by to pick you up and no one was home, I tried calling your cell, but it kept going right to voice mail. I just figured you'd forgotten about me." Curtis laughed and scratched at the back of his head. "I was mad at you all night. But if I'd just checked my freaking phone . . ."

Like I could ever forget about you, Lane thought.

Okay. It was time. Time to do this thing. Time to throw herself out there. *He'd be an idiot not to go out with you,* Jonathan's voice said in her mind. "Curtis—"

"I'm really sorry," he said. "Tonight was supposed to be fun, but instead it got all screwed up. But you should have been there. It was totally insane. This guy came wi—"

"Curtis," Lane attempted. But he was rambling.

"And then he set up a turntable and it was like something out of a bad movie. He was jus—"

"Curtis!"

He flinched. "What?"

Lane's heart stopped beating. She held her breath. "Will you go to the prom with me?"

Curtis's face went slack. The whole world slowed to a crawl. Lane's hopes and dreams washed away with the first few drops of rain. *Petrified* was the only word she could think of to describe his expression. Big, fat drops of rain smacked down on the crown of Lane's head, as if taunting her.

"Never mind," she said, backing up. "I don't know why I just said that. I—"

"Lane. Wait," Curtis said. He covered his face with both hands for a second, then dragged them down. "Dammit. It's not that I wouldn't want to go with you—"

"But you don't. That's fine. I get it," Lane was navigating backwards across her lawn as the raindrops came faster.

"No, it's just . . . I already have a date," Curtis said.

Lane felt as if a spotlight had just snapped on, searing her with its hot, white light. She imagined the entire AV squad from school—along with everyone else she knew—standing on Curtis's roof, training the light on her and laughing at her humiliation. She wanted to throw up. Right there on the driveway walk. This was supposed to be her night. The first day of the new Lane—the Lane who spoke up for herself and got what she wanted. Instead it was a nightmare.

"Of course. Of course you do," Lane said, still backing away. "I mean, the prom is next week already. And you have a tux. How could you not have a date?"

"Well, I didn't until tonight," Curtis said, looking physically ill. "I asked Kim Wolfe. At the party."

Lane lost all ability to breathe. Tonight? He'd asked Kim Wolfe *tonight*? When she was supposed to be with him. Tonight when she was out doing Vivi's dirty work Curtis had still been dateless. The realization of her missed opportunity hit her like a lightning bolt to the head. If only she had known where the party was, if only she had gotten there first . . .

"Kim Wolfe?" Lane said, her brain not quite functioning. "I didn't even know you two were—"

"We're not. I mean, we're not, like, dating or anything. I just—" Curtis made a frustrated noise in the back of his throat and shoved his hands under his arms. "Kim is—"

"A total gossip with a completely ridiculous love of the word *woot*?" Lane blurted. "Which, by the way, isn't even a word!"

Curtis pulled his head back, stunned. "Lane—"

"I have to go," Lane said, whipping around. Her soaked hair swung around and smacked her in the eye. She tripped over one of the sprinklers hidden in the lawn. Pain exploded in her toe, but she kept right on walking. Insult to major injury.

"Lane!"

"I'll talk to you later!" she said, attempting to sound normal through her tears. Hand shaking and wet, she managed to grasp the doorknob and shove her way into her house. Inside she leaned back against the door and dropped to the floor, clutching her injured toe and trying very, very hard not to cry.

"Thanks a lot, Jonathan," she muttered under her breath. It was his pep talk that had convinced her to do this. His confidence in her that had finally made her believe it would all go her way. Well, she'd finally done it. She'd finally spoken up for herself and put herself on the line.

And now she was sitting on a cold tile floor, dripping wet, with her bare toe throbbing in her hand, her heart breaking, and tears streaming down her face. So much for that.

✳ ✳ ✳

Lane pulled up right behind Vivi's car in Isabelle's driveway the following morning. Vivi was just getting out of her convertible. Lane's body temperature skyrocketed at the very sight of her friend.

It's all your fault, she thought, narrowing her eyes. *If you hadn't forced me to go over to Jonathan's on a pointless mission, I would have been with Curtis last night and he wouldn't have been anywhere near Kim "Woot-Woot" Wolfe.*

Vivi looked over at Lane impatiently, shoving her sunglasses up on her head. "Are you coming or are you just going to sit there keeping the seat warm?" she snapped.

Lane narrowed her eyes. Was *Vivi* mad at *her*? For what? For being a good little errand girl and driving all the way over to Cranston for her? Lane got out of the car, slammed the door, and stormed right past Vivi on the front walk. "She called you, too, huh?" she asked curtly.

"Of course she did. Why wouldn't she?" Vivi asked, scurrying up behind Lane.

"Oh, I don't know. Maybe she somehow sensed you were the cause of all her misery," Lane said over her shoulder, her heart pounding like crazy.

"Me! You're the one who went over there to convince him not to bail and failed miserably," Vivi replied, shoving her hand into the front pocket of her large hoodie. "Did you even try, Lane? I mean, really try?"

"Of course I did!" Lane shot back. She reached out and rang the bell. "But *someone* had already offended him so badly, he wants nothing to do with us!"

"Uh!" Vivi exclaimed indignantly, her mouth hanging open. "You have got a lot of—"

At that moment, the door swung open, and there stood Isabelle, makeupless and wearing her pink Victoria's Secret pj's, tears streaming from her swollen eyes. She had about five tissues crushed in each hand.

"H-h-hi guys!" she wailed.

Lane forgot all about Vivi and Curtis and Jonathan. She forgot everything. Never in her life had she seen Isabelle look so horrible. Guilt seeped in like cold lead around her heart.

"Iz?" Vivi said uncertainly.

Isabelle stepped forward and wrapped them both into her arms, snotting all over Lane's shoulder. "I'm s-s-so glad you're h-h-h-here!" she cried.

Lane looked at Vivi over Isabelle's bent head. *We did this to her,* she thought, narrowing her eyes.

Vivi rolled her eyes right back, telling her to back off.

Then Vivi extricated herself and closed the door. "Come on, Iz. Let's go sit down."

"Okay," Isabelle said with a sniffle.

She held one of the tissue wads to her nose as she shuffled between her friends toward the living room. On the couch in the normally pristine, opulent room, was a bowl of half-eaten cereal, three Pop-Tart wrappers, ten romantic tragedy DVDs, and Isabelle's laptop. Izzy shoved the Pop-Tart wrappers aside with her foot as she sat, and placed the bowl on the floor to make room for them, weeping the whole way.

"It's gonna be okay, Iz," Lane said, sitting down on the couch.

"No, it's not!" Isabelle wailed. "He dumped me! Everything was totally fine and then we went on a date and then he dumped me! Do you realize what this means?"

There was a lump in Lane's throat the size of a soccer ball.

"It means he thinks I'm repulsive!" Isabelle cried, throwing her hands up. A few of the tissues tumbled to the floor. "I'm hideous!"

"Isabelle, you're not hideous," Vivi said, reaching out to stroke Izzy's hair. "Come on, you know you're not hideous."

"Well, why else would he have dumped me?" Isabelle asked, wiping her face. "You guys were there! What did I do? Did I say something wrong? Did I offend him?"

Lane was growing so frustrated, she wanted to scream. She would kill to be able to tell her friend the truth. Of course she hadn't said anything wrong. The whole thing was a freaking lie! But she couldn't. Because then Isabelle would hate them both and she would throw them out and then she wouldn't even have any friends to cry to.

"You didn't say anything wrong," Lane told her, stacking the DVDs up neatly on the coffee table and swiping some crumbs off the couch. "I'm sure there's a good explanation."

"Well, I'd *love* to know what it is, but he won't write me back," Isabelle said as she pulled the computer onto her lap. She struck the keys haphazardly like she wanted to break the thing. "Why! Won't! He! Write! Me! Back!?" She said each word with another slam of a key.

Lane and Vivi's wide eyes met, disturbed. As angry as Lane was at Vivi, they were in this thing together. And this thing was getting serious.

"Okay, Iz, let's just leave the nice computer alone," Vivi said, pulling the laptop away from her and setting it on the side table. She closed it with a snap, and Isabelle looked at it longingly. "Listen, you don't need him," Vivi said. "He's just a guy."

"But what about the prom?" Isabelle asked, looking at Vivi, then Lane, wild eyed. "I have no date!"

"So we'll all go together. Alone, together," Vivi suggested, putting her hand over Isabelle's.

"Really?" Isabelle said hopefully.

"Yes! It's a perfect idea," Lane said, taking Isabelle's other hand. Her heart panged as she thought of Curtis. Of her failed attempt at happiness. But she managed an encouraging smile. "Who needs dates? We have each other."

"We have each other," Isabelle repeated, looking at each of them with such deep thanks in her eyes, Lane wanted to tear her own hair out. "You guys are the best friends in the world, you know that?"

Then she reached out and pulled them both to her so fast, she almost knocked Lane and Vivi's heads together.

"I could never get through this without you guys," Isabelle said dramatically.

Lane's heart squeezed in her chest. Little did Isabelle know she wouldn't even be going through this if it *weren't* for them. She reached up and around Isabelle's shoulder and patted her awkwardly on the back.

"We know," she said, feeling like a total jerk. "We know."

★★ nineteen ★★

Vivi paced back and forth in front of the picture window in her living room, holding up the skirt of her floor-length black dress with both hands. Every few steps, her ankle turned in her high heels. She finally dropped onto the couch to yank them off. Why everyone seemed to feel the need to wear those torture devices was beyond her. She thought longingly of her black Converse lying on the floor of her room and wondered if anyone would notice if she wore them instead.

"She's late. Why is she so late?" Vivi asked Lane. "Did I not say pictures at six? You were here at six. Curtis *told* me he was going to be late because Kim had a dance recital thing this afternoon, but Isabelle said nothing. Where the heck *is* she?"

In the kitchen, her mother and Lane's parents chatted over drinks, waiting for the rest of the group to arrive. Their laughter was mocking Vivi's anxiety.

"Will you calm down already?" Lane said through her teeth. "You're making me tense."

"I'm just worried, all right?" Vivi said, looking out the window as a car rolled by. "What if she cracked? What if she decided she couldn't handle going without a date and she's curled up in a ball on her floor right now?"

"I'm sure she's not," Lane said, looking rather piqued anyway.

"Text her," Vivi said, crossing her arms over her chest.

"Why do I have to text her?" Lane asked.

"Because your bag and phone are right there and mine are upstairs," Vivi shot back. Why was Lane being so difficult lately?

Lane rolled her eyes and snatched her purse off the couch. "Fine."

Vivi stood there, tapping her foot as Lane texted Isabelle. While they waited for a reply, her mother came up behind her.

"Anyone else get here yet?" her mom asked.

"Not yet," Vivi trilled, sarcastically matching her mother's happy tone.

"Oh, honey. You look so beautiful," Vivi's mother said, snatching her up into a tight hug. "Have I said how fabulous I think it is that you have the confidence to go to your prom without a date?"

Vivi's heart panged. "You've mentioned it."

"Well, I do. I think if there's no one in your life who you think is worthy of sharing such a night with, it's a wise decision to go on your own terms," her mother told her, touching her face. "I'm so proud of you."

Vivi attempted a smile as her mother moved away. She wouldn't be so proud if she knew that she'd given up her chance at a dream date so that Isabelle could have one instead. Which wouldn't even be so bad if that whole thing hadn't backfired as well. What a waste.

Suddenly, Lane's phone beeped. Vivi stood next to her so they could both read it.

> **Isabelle:** Sorry so late. Mom wanted 2 tk some pix in R yard. Just me & my date!!!

Vivi's heart hit the floor. "Her *date*?"

"What date?" Lane blurted.

"Ask her!" Vivi demanded.

Lane texted back.

> **Lane:** What date?

It took Isabelle about two seconds to reply.

> **Isabelle:** It's a surprise!!! On r way now!!!

"Omigod. She's going with Sluttig! I know it! This is a nightmare!" Vivi exclaimed, shoving her hands into her hair. She paced to the window and back, feeling like a caged dog.

"We don't know that," Lane said.

"Who else could it be? Why would she have kept it a secret from us unless it was Shawn?" Vivi demanded, crossing her arms over her stomach. "I can't believe this. I can't believe that after everything we've done she ended up with Sluttig anyway."

How could this be happening? How had everything gotten so very far out of her control?

Just then, Vivi heard footsteps on the stairs and looked up to find her brother descending in a full tuxedo. His blond hair was gelled, but casually—not into a helmet like he used to wear it—and he looked very handsome. There was just one problem.

"What the hell do you think you're doing?" Vivi demanded.

"Going to the prom," Marshall replied, adjusting his lapels with a smile.

"Uh, Marshall, I hate to break it to you, but you're not a senior," Vivi said.

"I told him he could be my plus-one," Lane said, stepping forward.

"What?" Vivi blurted.

"Wow, Marshall. Very James Bond," Lane said appreciatively, dusting some lint off his shoulder.

"Thanks," Marshall said, turning around and striking a pose. "Swayne. Marshall Swayne."

"Dork. Major dork," Vivi amended.

"Vivi. What is your problem?" Lane asked.

"My problem?" Vivi said, pacing. "My problem is we're supposed to be going without dates, remember? We made a pact! We promised Isabelle."

"I'm not really her date," Marshall explained.

"Yeah, I just thought he should get to go. You know, after all the work we forced him to do," Lane replied. "And besides, Isabelle has a date now, so—"

"She does?" Marshall asked.

"Yeah, which means I'm the only one without one!" Vivi blurted.

Out of the corner of her eye, Vivi saw the stretch Mercedes limo pull up in front of her house. This was it. Everything had officially spiraled out of her control.

"They're here!" she shouted to her mother, just because she felt an extreme need to shout.

She and Lane and Marshall all fell to their knees on the couch to see out. The parents, meanwhile, headed right for the front door to greet the newcomers.

"I cannot wait to see Isabelle's dress," Lane's mother said as she click-clacked by in her heels. "That girl has always had the most impeccable taste."

"Except when it comes to guys," Vivi said quietly, feeling nauseated. "I swear on my life, if Shawn Sluttig gets out of that car . . ."

Isabelle's father's silver Infiniti pulled up behind the limo and her parents got out. Then, the back door of the limo opened and out stepped . . .

Jonathan Hess.

"Jonathan?" Vivi gasped without even thinking. She couldn't have formed another coherent thought if she'd tried. Jonathan was here. And if a Hollywood scout had driven by at that moment, he would have been snatched up and dropped on a red carpet within twenty-four hours. He looked gorgeous. Sleek black tux. Long gray tie. Sexily tousled hair. Perfection. He walked around the back of the car and opened the door for Izzy. Vivi suddenly couldn't watch anymore. She turned around and flopped down on the couch. "But how . . . ?"

"I guess something I said convinced him," Lane said giddily.

Vivi felt as if nothing would ever make sense again. "I guess it did," she said dubiously. "But why didn't she tell us he changed his mind? The girl was devastated all week. You'd think she would have told us he was coming. Why didn't she—?"

"Who cares?" Lane trilled, her eyes bright. "He's here! *Brandon* came through! Oh my God, Vivi! It worked! Isabelle has her dream date!"

Just like that, it was like all the tension between Lane and Vivi faded away. It hadn't all been for nothing. All the debating, all the plotting, all the angst. It had actually worked.

Out in the foyer, Vivi's mother and Lane's parents greeted Isabelle and her family and Jonathan.

"Oh, Isabelle! How lovely you look!" Lane's mother gushed.

"Just like a princess right out of a Shakespeare play," Vivi's mother agreed.

"And who is this handsome young man?" Lane's mom asked.

"Brandon. Nice to meet you."

Vivi's brain went foggy at the sound of his voice. She felt weak. Jonathan was not supposed to be here. He was not supposed to be standing in her house looking runway-worthy with her best friend at his side.

"Wrap your brain around it, Vivi. You should be psyched!" Lane said. "Your plan worked. She's not with Shawn. You did it!"

"We did it," Marshall corrected.

Vivi took a deep breath. Lane was right. This was a moment for celebration. They had actually pulled it off. Isabelle was happy. She was going to the prom with the guy of her dreams. Vivi just wished that the guy wasn't also the guy of her own dreams. But beggars could not be choosers.

"You're right," she said finally, smoothing her dress down. She cleared her throat, shook her hair back, and resolved to put her feelings aside for the rest of the night. This was for Isabelle. It was all about Isabelle. And maybe, just maybe, everything would be all right. "Come on," she told her coconspirators. "Let's get this soap opera on the road."

How the heck did I end up here? Vivi thought as the unrelenting sun beat down on her face. She stood in the center of the yard, flanked on one side by Isabelle the Pink Princess and Jonathan the Movie God, and by Happy Little Lane and Always-in-Vivi's-Face Marshall on the other. If someone had told her three years ago that she'd be going to the prom dateless while one of her best friends went with her brother and the other went with the guy Vivi was seriously crushing on, she would have decked that person. But here she was. And the more Jonathan made Isabelle giggle and preen, the more Vivi seriously considered changing into a T-shirt and hitting the basement with a pint of ice cream and an X-Men movie marathon.

No. Even they were too romantic. Maybe zombie movies.

"Hey, everyone! Happy prom!" Curtis announced, bursting through the back door and out onto the lawn.

"Woot! Woot!" Kim Wolfe cheered, pumping her palms in the air in her garish green dress.

Vivi's stomach turned and she looked at Lane, who had completely lost her smile. Okay. So maybe Happy Little Lane hadn't been the worst thing. Depressed Lane was going to suck. Curtis and Kim's parents appeared at the back door behind them, and Vivi's mom and the other parents rushed to greet them.

"How's it going, man?" Curtis asked, slapping hands with Marshall. Curtis was wearing a black tux and a red tie with colorful swirling designs all over it. It would have looked silly on anyone else, but on Curtis it was just cute. "Hey, Vivi," he said, putting his hands in his pockets. "Lane," he added somewhat awkwardly.

"Hi," Lane said. Just then Kim sidled up to him and slipped her arm around his.

"Hi, all!" she trilled.

Lane turned around and headed for the patio. "I need some lemonade."

Curtis looked at Vivi uncertainly, but before she could even think of something to say, Isabelle came over to introduce Jonathan.

"Curtis, Kim, this is Brandon," Izzy said.

"Nice to meet you," Jonathan said, shaking hands with them.

"You too," Curtis said.

And then, awkward silence ensued.

"Well, I'm thirsty too!" Curtis said finally. "Who wants a drink?"

"I'm in!" Isabelle said.

Then they turned and lead the group up to the patio, where Lane was sitting in a chair, sipping sweetened lemonade with a look on her face that was all sour. With Isabelle's back turned, Vivi saw her chance. She grabbed Jonathan's arm and pulled him behind the huge rhododendron by the back fence.

"Vivi! What are you doing? Isabelle's gonna be suspicious," Jonathan protested.

"I don't care. We have to talk," Vivi said.

Jonathan looked like a caged rabbit. All darting eyes and shifty feet. "About what?"

"Well, first of all, thanks for coming," Vivi said. "After the way we left things—"

"Yeah, well, *Lane* was very convincing," Jonathan said.

Vivi felt a pang. It wasn't like she expected him to say he needed to see *her* again, but it still, somehow, hurt.

"Okay. Well, good," Vivi said, her hands on her hips.

"Can I go now?" Jonathan looked extremely uncomfortable.

"No! Wait! We never had a chance to go over what happens next," Vivi said, her heart pounding in her ears.

Jonathan's brow creased. Even that was gorgeous. "What happens next?"

"Yeah. What you're going to say . . . you know . . . to let her down easy," Vivi said, feeling disgusted with herself. She knew he hated this stuff, the lying and scheming, but she had to do it.

"No one expects you to play Brandon forever. The deal was you take her to the prom. So we had an idea of what you could say to let her know you won't be seeing her again after tonight."

Jonathan looked incredulous for a moment, but he stood up straight and focused on her. "I'm all ears."

"We were thinking you could tell her you're going away for the summer to a conservatory or something. To study music. Someplace far away," Vivi explained quickly. "Tell her it's a serious immersion program and you're not supposed to have any distractions like e-mail or anything."

"Seriously? That's your plan?" Jonathan's tone was mocking.

"What? She'll love that you're so dedicated to your music. You can just tell her that you've loved knowing her, but you need to focus on your future. It's just like every crappy romance novel she's ever read. She devours them at a rate of two a day down the shore every summer," Vivi told him. "They're her guilty pleasure."

"Okay. So I'm going to a conservatory in a foreign country where I can't have access to e-mail," Jonathan said. "Fine. But if she buys that, she's not as smart as you guys have always made her out to be."

Wow. He really wasn't giving her an inch here.

"It'll work," Vivi said defensively. "I know her a little bit better than you do."

"Fine," Jonathan said. "We should go before they realize we're both missing. When's your date getting here?"

Vivi's stomach hollowed out. "I don't have a date, remember?"

She hated the almost hopeful tone of her voice, but it was too late to take it back now. And she was hopeful. Hopeful he'd do something. Take her in his arms. Kiss her. Tell her he wished he were here with her instead of Izzy. Anything.

But his beautiful face was blank. "Oh yeah. Right. Well." And that was it. He turned around and slipped back out into the yard, leaving Vivi there alone to hold back her tears.

Dancing in the center of the country club dance floor, surrounded by her classmates, Lane felt as if she had to be dreaming. It couldn't be her senior prom. How had it come so quickly? One second she was a freshman looking up at the tall, confident seniors in awe, and now she was a senior and she didn't feel confident or awe-inspiring, let alone tall. She had thought that by the time she was a senior things would be different. She'd be cool and secure, totally certain of who she was and where she was going—just like all those older girls had seemed to her when she first started high school. But now here she was, a month away from graduation, dancing at the prom with her friend's little brother because she couldn't get a date with the guy she wanted to go with. The guy who was currently grinding with Kim Wolfe on the other side of the dance floor.

Lane danced around Marshall until her back was facing

Curtis. That was something she did not need to see. At least she was certain of that much.

"Having fun?" she asked Marshall.

He managed to nod as he continued to step back and forth to the music—one of those sucky dance versions of a formerly poignant love song that Lane just hated. Unfortunately, if the last two sets were any indication, the DJ seemed to love them. "Sorry. I'm not the greatest dancer," Marshall said.

"You're way better than most of the guys here," Lane told him. "At least you can find a beat."

Marshall grinned. "Yeah. I guess that's good."

"Omigod, Lane, *who* is that guy with Isabelle?" Jenny Lang asked, grabbing Lane's arm.

"His name's Brandon. He's from Connecticut," Lane lied.

"Damn. I wish I'd applied to UConn. I mean if they grow 'em like that up there," Jenny said, blushing. "He is totally the hottest guy here." Her eyes flicked at Marshall. "No offense."

"None taken," Marshall shouted to be heard over the music.

"*Look* at them!" Jenny said, her eyes wide. "He's all over her! How long have they been going out?"

All over her? Lane thought, confused. She glanced over at Isabelle and Jonathan, and, sure enough, they were standing in the middle of the dance floor, locked together. Instead of dancing to the semi-insane beat like the rest of the crowd, they were moving slowly back and forth, staring deeply into each other's eyes. Jonathan's hand moved up and down Isabelle's back. She sighed, closed her eyes, and leaned her cheek against her chest.

"Uh . . . not that long," Lane answered finally.

"Well, they are clearly in love," Jenny said. "Everyone's talking about it."

"Really?" Lane asked.

"Are you kidding? No one ever understood what she was doing with Shawn Littig. Good for her. Ciao!" Jenny said before disappearing into the crowd again.

"Are you okay?" Marshall asked Lane.

"*What* is going on over there?" Lane asked him under his breath. "They look like long-lost lovers or something."

Marshall glanced over, then cleared his throat and quickly looked away. "Well, maybe he's just playing it up."

"No one told him to do *that,*" Lane gasped as Jonathan's hand grazed Izzy's butt.

Isabelle looked up at Jonathan, startled, but then they both laughed. Isabelle was completely glowing. Her face was flushed; her eyes were bright. She was a total goner.

"Omigod, you guys!" Vivi trilled, weaving through the crowded dance floor to join them. "Have you *seen* Sluttig? He's totally green!"

Vivi lifted her hand to point Shawn out, but it took a moment for Lane to find him. That was because he wasn't on the dance floor, but sitting at a table on the edge of it, slumped down, staring at Isabelle and Jonathan with murderous eyes.

"Probably doesn't help that Tricia Blank has had her tongue down Dell Landry's throat all night," Marshall pointed out, nodding toward the corner, where Tricia was curled up in the quarterback's lap.

"Definitely not." Vivi laughed, swiping her long blond hair over her shoulder.

"I just hope Shawn doesn't start something with Jonathan," Lane said. "I don't think he signed up for an ER trip."

"Eh. He'll be fine," Vivi said. "I'm sure he can hold his own." For the first time, she looked over at the couple she'd engineered, and her face completely fell. Lane's heart went with it. She knew that Vivi was seeing what *she* was seeing. Two people who were totally falling for each other.

"Vivi," Lane started to say.

"You know what?" Vivi interrupted, recovering herself. She lifted her arm, her sleek silver camera dangling from a strap on her wrist. "I think I'm going to go take a picture of Shawn to record this for posterity."

Lane sighed as Vivi rushed off. She wished the girl could just admit how she felt about Jonathan already. But really, from the way things looked now, there might be little to no point. Jonathan touched Isabelle's face with his fingertips as they danced, still gazing into her eyes.

"This is unbelievable," Lane said, looking up at Marshall— who was staring longingly at Isabelle and Jonathan.

Suddenly Lane recalled all the times she and Izzy had been over at his house and he had attempted to join in on the conversation, only to be thwarted by Vivi. She remembered how great he'd been the night Izzy had found out about Shawn's cheating, bringing Izzy her favorite root beer. She realized how nervous he'd been at the idea of IMing with Isabelle at first, but how obsessed he'd become with it once he'd gotten started. And then there were the new clothes, the new haircut, the fact that he'd shown up at Isabelle's first date with "Brandon." He'd been there to check Jonathan out. To size up the person who was taking his place with Isabelle. And then it hit her.

"Oh my God. Marshall! You like Isabelle!" Lane gasped.

"What? No, I don't," Marshall said quickly. He blushed and looked away.

The dance song ended and a slow one began. Half the people vacated the dance floor, but Lane clung to Marshall.

"Yes, you do!" she whispered. "You were just totally staring at her! I know that look! You like Izzy!"

"I do not!" Marshall said through his teeth.

"I can*not* believe I didn't see this before," Lane said, grinning. "Marshall, why don't you—?"

"Lane, I don't like Isabelle, okay?" He sighed in frustration and looked around to see if anyone was in earshot, then ducked his head closer to hers. "Can you keep a secret?"

"Of course," Lane replied.

Marshall took a deep breath. For a brief second, he dug his teeth into his bottom lip, and then he blurted it out. "I wasn't staring at Isabelle. I was staring at Jonathan."

Lane stopped dancing.

"I'm gay, Lane," Marshall whispered, averting his eyes. "But you can't tell anyone. Especially not Vivi. You have to swear."

"I swear," Lane said, breathless. She wasn't completely shocked. Just shocked that she was the first person he told. And that he liked Jonathan. One more tangle for their big old web.

Marshall dropped his arms and blew out a sigh. "Maybe we should take a break."

"Sounds like a plan," Lane said, eager to sit for a second and collect her thoughts.

She turned around to head off the dance floor and nearly bumped right into Curtis. Curtis standing there in his perfect tux and his funky red tie, all alone. Lane's heart pounded painfully, and she looked around for an escape. But then Curtis opened his arms and raised his eyebrows. "Shall we?"

"Sure," Lane managed to say.

She could hardly even look at him as he wrapped his arms around her waist and started to move. She was too embarrassed, too tense, too everything. She glanced at him, found him staring right at her, then flinched and quickly looked away.

Say something! Say anything! Lane chided herself.

"I like your dress," Curtis said finally.

"Thanks. You picked out a good tux," Lane replied.

"I thought it was me."

"Well, it is."

"Good."

"Good."

There was a long moment of silence as they continued to dance. Lane was just starting to wonder if this damn song was ever going to end so that she could breathe again, when Curtis spoke.

"Lane, there's something I want to tell you," he said. He stopped dancing.

The entire world went quiet. For a split second, everything

was still. Lane knew whatever he said next was going to change her life. Somehow knew it with complete certainty. He was either going to break her heart or make her year. She looked into his warm brown eyes and braced herself.

"Yeah?"

"I just want you to know that—"

"Curtis! Come on!" Kim appeared out of nowhere and grabbed Curtis's arm. "They're taking our table picture! We can't not be in it! Woot woot!"

She yanked Curtis away and he tripped, staring back at Lane with an apology in his eyes. Just like that, the whole world came rushing back—loud music, laughing voices, bad perfume—and Lane had missed her moment once again.

twenty

Vivi slid all the way to the end of the seat in the limousine and stared out the window. If she had to watch Izzy and Jonathan make lovey-dovey eyes at each other for one more minute, she seriously might die of misery.

God, I wish I could skip the post-prom party, she thought to herself as her friends took their dear, sweet time getting in the car. But she couldn't. She had to be there when Jonathan broke up with Isabelle. *If* he broke up with her. From the looks of things, those two could very well be headed toward promise rings and two-point-five kids.

"Hey!" Curtis whispered, tapping her arm as he followed her in. "Operation Skewer Sluttig is in full effect, huh? Isabelle's loving that guy!"

Vivi's stomach turned. "Yeah. Great."

Curtis shot her a confused look and took the seat across the way. He was quickly joined by Kim, who was scrolling through the pictures on her digital camera. Marshall sat next to her and Lane squeezed in next to him, which left the space next to Vivi open for the couple of the century. Jonathan sat down right next to Vivi, his thigh grazing hers, and she pressed herself even closer to the window.

Kill me. Just kill me now.

"What are you doing all the way over there?" Jonathan said to Isabelle as soon as the door was closed. Vivi watched in horror as he pulled Isabelle up onto his lap and she giggled happily, her prom queen crown slightly askew.

"Brandon!" she teased, slapping his shoulder. She did not, however, move off him. Instead she kicked her silver shoes off and they promptly slammed into Vivi's feet.

"Yeah! Woot! Woot!" Kim Wolfe cheered, climbing into Curtis's lap as well.

Vivi stared at Lane across the wide expanse of the car. The plan was working, but somehow, this night could not get any worse.

"Driver! To Dell Landry's!" Isabelle called out cheerily.

"Yes, ma'am!" the driver replied.

Luckily, it was a short ride, and Kim filled the time by passing around her camera and making everyone look at her "awesome" pictures, most of which were of her random friends striking slutty modeling poses on the dance floor. Jonathan and Izzy, however, ignored her pleas to take the camera, whispering and giggling with one another, Jonathan's arms locked around Isabelle's tiny waist. When the limo finally pulled up the wide driveway to their classmate's sprawling home, Vivi had to press her fingernails into her palms to keep from clawing her way out.

"Are you okay?" Lane asked Vivi, falling into step with her as she beelined it for the front door and the mayhem inside.

"I'm fine. Totally, totally fine," Vivi said, her fists clenched.

"You guys! Wait up!" Isabelle called after them, jogging in her long skirt and high heels. Vivi didn't slow, but Izzy caught up with them anyway. "Omigod, you guys. How amazing is Brandon?"

Lane shot Vivi a pained look. Vivi appreciated the sympathy, even as it irritated her. All she wanted was to get the heck out of there.

"So amazing," Lane said, touching Izzy's arm.

"The way he looks into my eyes? You guys, it's so incredible!" Isabelle gushed as they crowded through the door. "I know this sounds insane, but I think he's going to tell me he loves me."

"What!?" Vivi blurted, stopping in the middle of the marble foyer. A bunch of kids who were already milling around with champagne and beer stopped to stare at them, but quickly saw nothing interesting was going on and got back to their cavorting. "You barely know each other," Vivi said.

"I know, but he's been hinting around about it all night," Isabelle gushed, hand to her heart. "Like he keeps saying there's something he really wants to tell me. And that he's never met anyone like me. And his voice gets all husky and I swear it just makes me gooey inside. It's so intense."

Vivi glanced back through the open door and saw that Marshall, Curtis, and Jonathan were all posing for a picture for Kim, Jonathan wearing his "I'm too cool as Brandon" smirk. What she wouldn't give to smack it right off his fickle face. Hadn't he just told Vivi that he liked *her*, like, a week ago?

"And you know what the really weird thing is?" Isabelle said. She looked around, grabbed each of their arms, and pulled them toward the wall, behind a huge potted plant. Vivi stared at her breathless friend, petrified to know what was coming next. "The weird thing is," Isabelle repeated, her brown eyes all dreamy, "that I think I love him, too."

"Isabelle," Lane said, her tone anguished.

Vivi's throat completely closed.

"Thank you guys *so* much for convincing me to come with him!" Isabelle gave them a quick hug and rushed over to throw herself into Jonathan's waiting arms.

"I'm the devil," Vivi said under her breath. "I'm so the devil."

"It's okay," Lane said. "It's gonna be okay."

But Vivi suddenly felt her chicken marsala was not quite sitting right in her stomach. She turned around, shoved Kim Wolfe aside, and sprinted for the bathroom.

"Go, Curtis! Go, Curtis! Go! Go! Go, Curtis!"

Vivi, Lane, and Isabelle all sat on one of the leather couches in Dell's living room, laughing their way to tears as Curtis solo-danced atop the slate coffee table. He'd lost his jacket, his tie was tied around his head, and his shirt was completely untucked. All around him, their tipsy classmates raised their arms and cheered him on. With Jonathan and Marshall nowhere to be seen, Vivi was more relaxed than she'd been all night. She wished her friends had stuck to the no-date rule. If they'd been alone like this all night, she might have actually had fun.

"Okay, what is happening right now?" Isabelle asked, laughing.

Lane giggled. "I think we're seeing drunk Curtis in *full effect*," she said, putting on a skater boy voice.

"Why do I not have a video camera?" Vivi wailed through her laughter. "This is prime blackmail material."

Suddenly Curtis jumped off the table and attempted a flying split. Which only split his pants. Everyone cracked up and cheered even louder as Curtis's face turned purple.

"It's not funny!" Curtis shouted, even as he laughed. "This is a rental!"

Lane doubled over laughing. Isabelle wiped tears from her eyes. Vivi watched them and tried to solidify this memory in her mind. Her one fun memory from her senior prom.

"You guys, this has been the best night ever," Isabelle said with a content sigh, sitting back as she got her laughter under control.

Instantly, Vivi's shoulders tensed. She knew from Isabelle's dreamy tone that she was thinking about Jonathan. The last thing Vivi wanted to be thinking about.

Isabelle looked up and her smile widened. "And it's only going to get better." Vivi's heart thumped. Jonathan had just walked into the room and was weaving his way toward them.

Isabelle struggled to push herself up off the sunken couch as he approached and he rushed the last few steps to take her arms and help her. Izzy tripped into him and giggled and Jonathan hugged her tenderly. Vivi suddenly felt like taking her shoe off and throwing it at him. It would be the first useful thing the damn heels had done for her all night.

"Where have you been?" Isabelle asked, blinking up at Jonathan. "I missed you!"

"I missed you, too," he said in a low, sexy voice, running his fingers across her cheek. "Can we . . . maybe . . . go outside?" he asked, glancing at Vivi and Lane like he wanted privacy.

"Absolutely," Isabelle said with a smile.

Jonathan started for the door, but Isabelle quickly turned around and grinned, giddy as could be.

Vivi's heart and stomach switched places in her body, which was not a pleasant feeling. "Do you think he's going to break up with her or tell her he loves her?"

"Vivi, there's no way he loves her. He hardly knows her," Lane said.

"Yeah, but I hardly know him and—"

Vivi stopped, a few words short of saying way too much. Lane, however, read her face like a book.

"Omigod. Vivi!" Lane moaned, realizing what Vivi had been about to confess. "This is like a Greek tragedy!"

Vivi's heart felt as if it might shrivel up and die. She couldn't just sit here and feel this.

"Come on." Vivi got up from the couch and grabbed Lane's hand.

"Come on where?" Lane asked in trepidation.

"I have to see what's happening," Vivi said, feeling panicked. She squeezed Lane's hand so hard, it was like their skin fused.

"Okay. Okay. Let's go," Lane replied.

Holding hands, they rushed across the living room and out the front door. Dozens of kids were hanging out under the stars, sipping their drinks or making out under and up against the huge oak trees that lined the drive.

"Where are they?" Vivi said through her teeth.

"There," Lane whispered, pointing.

Isabelle and Jonathan were huddled close together near the bubbling fountain a few yards away. Vivi would have given anything to be able to hear what they were saying, but between the party noise and the running water, she never would have been able to eavesdrop without being right on top of them.

"Over here." Vivi pulled Lane toward one of the columns outside the front door. She positioned her friend across from her and tried to keep an eye on the proceedings. "Try to make it look like we're just chatting."

"Ooookay . . . So, can you believe that awful mermaid-from-hell dress Kim Wolfe is wearing?" Lane said, clearly trying to lighten the mood. She glanced over at Izzy and Jonathan.

"Omigod. I know. You are about a hundred times hotter than her," Vivi said quickly. She had to keep reminding herself to breathe.

"Really? Thanks," Lane said. "I wish Curtis would—"

"Hang on," Vivi said, touching Lane's arm to stop her.

Across the way, Isabelle's eyes widened. Vivi wasn't a lip-reader, but she knew what the word *what* looked like, and that's what Isabelle kept saying. Jonathan reached out to touch her arm and Isabelle let him, but then she lifted her hands to her face. Vivi's heart turned to stone.

"Oh, God. Is she—," Lane began.

"She's crying," Vivi said. "Oh my God! She's *sobbing*!"

Jonathan said a few pleading words and Isabelle nodded quickly, but the tears kept coming. And even as Vivi's heart went out to her friend, she couldn't help feeling just the slightest bit relieved. He wasn't telling Isabelle he loved her. There was still a chance—

Oh my God. I am *the devil,* Vivi thought, sick to her stomach.

"This is awful," Lane said, turning away. "She thought he was going to tell her he loved her and instead he's breaking up with her."

Vivi attempted to swallow but couldn't. Her vision blurred with tears. This was wrong. It was all so, so wrong.

Then, Jonathan and Isabelle hugged. They hugged for a long, long time, Izzy's face turned to the side, her eyes squeezed closed.

Finally Jonathan pulled back and wiped his thumb across Isabelle's cheek, drying her tears. Vivi felt like her own heart was tearing open. His touch was so tender. So reverent. She cold practically feel his fingertips on her own skin.

"I can't watch this," Vivi said, turning away.

"It's okay," Lane said. "They're hugging again."

"Again?" The pain was excruciating.

"Yeah, and now he's going. They're saying good-bye. This is good, right? I mean, sort of," Lane said hopefully.

Vivi's breath caught and she looked up again. Sure enough, Jonathan was backing down the driveway toward a cab that was waiting at the far end, past all the haphazardly parked cars. He watched Isabelle the whole way as Izzy stood there, her shoulders shaking with her sobs.

He's going. This is it. Vivi felt as if her heart were being pulled right out of her chest. *I'm never going to see him again. And I don't even get to say good-bye.*

At the very last second, Jonathan looked up. Looked right at Vivi. Her heart stopped beating. She just needed him to nod at her. Or wave. Anything to show her that he still cared about her. But he just looked up at the house, and Vivi was suddenly uncertain whether he'd seen her there at all. Then he turned and was gone.

And just like that, tears were streaming down her face.

"She's alone. Come on," Lane said to Vivi, grabbing her wrist.

"I can't," Vivi cried.

Lane looked at her and her jaw dropped. "You're crying!"

"No, I'm not!" Vivi said, using her palms to quickly dry her face. "I'm fine."

"Vivi—"

Vivi's heart cracked at Lane's sympathetic tone. And she just started to babble. "It's just . . . you guys were right. I do push guys I really like away. That's what I do! Because they're not good enough or I'm scared of . . . of not having control or whatever. But this time, he *was* good enough. He *so* was, Lane. And what did I do? I not only pushed him away, I pushed him right at my best friend!"

"Oh, Vivi," Lane said. "I'm sorry. I didn't want to be right." She reached over and hugged Vivi, and Vivi clung to her, trying to get control of her breathing.

"He's gone," Vivi said. "And he hates me."

"Vivi, I'm really sorry. I *know* this sucks. But we have to talk to Isabelle," Lane said firmly, pulling away. "We did this to her. We need to be there for her right now."

"I can't," Vivi repeated, shaking her head as the tears continued to come.

"You *have* to!" Lane said. "Now come on."

Vivi took a deep breath and nodded. Lane grabbed her hand and squeezed as they headed down the driveway.

"Isabelle!" Lane called out. "Isabelle. What happened?"

"You guys!" Isabelle threw herself into Lane's arms. "He's gone! Brandon's gone!"

Vivi turned away and dried her face again, sucking in a big gulp of air to steady herself. She had to be strong right now. For Isabelle.

"Gone?" Lane improvised. "Oh, you mean he went home?"

"No. I mean he's gone. He's leaving for a conservatory in Paris tomorrow morning. He's gonna be there all summer," Isabelle cried. "I can't believe this! I thought we were going to be together and he just . . . he just . . . broke up with me!"

"Iz, I'm so sorry," Vivi said, feeling lower than she ever had in her life.

"But it's not like he didn't like you," Lane pointed out.

"He probably just thinks long-distance relationships don't work."

Isabelle's eyes widened. "That's exactly what he said! And I believe him. I do," she said, pacing away and toying with her clutch purse. "It's just I wish it didn't hurt so much. I'm never going to see him again!" she wailed, fresh tears streaming down her face.

Tell me about it, Vivi thought.

"C'mere," Vivi said to Isabelle. She hugged her friend as she cried, her own tears hidden behind Isabelle's back. "It's okay, Iz. It's gonna be okay. Sooner or later, this whole thing is just going to be a distant memory."

Lane stepped over and made it a group hug, her head bent to Vivi's shoulder, like she was comforting Vivi as much as she was comforting Isabelle.

"I'm just gonna miss him," Isabelle sniffled, putting her chin on Vivi's shoulder. "I'm gonna miss him so much."

Join the club, Vivi thought, reaching up to wipe a tear from under her own eye. She knew exactly how Izzy felt.

★ ★ twenty-one ★ ★

"I still can't believe Curtis split his pants." Vivi doubled over laughing as she and Lane sat at a table in Lonnie's the following morning. All around them their classmates sipped their coffees, everyone in comfy sweats or jeans, chatting about the night before. "I wonder if the rental place will take them back."

Lane tried to laugh, but couldn't. Her heart was way too heavy. "Do you think they hooked up?" she asked.

Vivi raised her eyebrows. "Who?"

"Curtis and Kim? Do you think they, like, made out?" Lane asked, pushing her coffee back and forth between her hands.

"I thought we agreed not to talk about anything depressing." Vivi glowered.

"Oh my God! You *do* think they hooked up!" Lane exclaimed.

"Uh, no," Vivi said. "No way. Curtis has better taste than that."

"He asked her to the prom, didn't he?" Lane pointed out.

"Only because you didn't ask him first," Vivi said. "I told you to—"

"Please do not go there right now," Lane interrupted, her shoulders tensing. She could not get into that particular conversation with Vivi. She wanted to try to keep today light.

"Fine," Vivi said, rolling her eyes. "Where is Isabelle?" she looked at the door. "That girl is never late."

"You don't think she's sitting around in sweats with Pop-Tarts again, do you?" Lane asked warily.

Vivi snorted. "Maybe she's with Shawn. You know, rebounding."

Lane laughed at the suggestion, but then her eyes locked with Vivi's and her stomach dropped. "She couldn't."

Vivi paled. "If all we did was drive her right back into Sluttig's arms . . ."

"We never should have done this," Lane said, holding her head in her hands. "I mean, could it have backfired any worse?"

"Hey! It did not backfire," Vivi said under her breath, leaning across the table. "The whole point was to keep her from going to the prom with Shawn, and she did not go to the prom with Shawn."

"I thought the whole point was to keep her from getting her heart broken again," Lane countered. "And instead, we just broke it for her. And yours, by the way."

Vivi sat back. "My heart is not broken," she said evasively. She picked up her bagel and ripped off a huge chunk with her teeth. "This was never about me. It was about Isabelle," she said through a mouthful of food.

"That's it. I'm calling her," Lane said, diving into her phone for her bag.

Just then, Vivi's phone beeped. "That must be her," Vivi said, producing her own phone from the pocket on her zipped hoodie. She read the text aloud.

"She says, 'You're never going to guess where I am,'" Vivi said, her brow wrinkling.

Lane got up and dropped down next to Vivi on the bench so she could see. Vivi typed back.

> **Vivi:** U'r supposed 2 B @ Lonnie's!!!
> **Isabelle:** cant make it. Im going to paris to surprise Brandon. Have noon flight. Am at Newark airport right now! Bought tix w/graduation $$!

"What?" Vivi shouted, silencing half of Lonnie's.

Lane's vision clouded over and she gripped the sides of the table. "Text her back! Text her back!"

Vivi typed furiously.

> **Vivi:** NO! You cant go to paris!
> **Isabelle:** Nvr felt this way B4! Have to go. Looked up his school on web and will be there 2nite!

"Do something!" Lane squealed. "Do anything!"

"I'm trying!" Vivi shouted.

> **Vivi:** DO NOT GET ON THAT PLANE!!!
> **Isabelle:** this is true love Viv. Crazy but true. Gotta go!
> **Vivi:** NO! Stop! Need 2 talk first.

Isabelle: guy @ metal detector needs to search stuff. Turn phone off now. Will call u when I land. Bye!!!

"Vivi! What are we going to do?" Lane screeched. Her heart pounded so hard, it drowned out all the Lonnie's noise around her.

Vivi's eyes darted around without focusing. "I . . . I . . ."

"This is not happening. This is so not happening," Lane rambled. She got up and paced next to the table, ignoring the disturbed looks of her classmates. "Do you realize what we've just done? Our best friend is getting on a plane to chase after a guy that doesn't even exist! A guy that we made up! We have to do something!"

With quaking hands, Vivi started dialing on her phone. "I'm calling her."

"She said she was turning off her phone!" Lane said.

"I have to try!" Vivi's hand clung to her hair, holding it back from her face. "Pick up, dammit! Pick up!"

Vivi stared up at Lane. "Voice mail," she said.

"Say something!" Lane demanded.

"Uh . . . Isabelle. It's Vivi. We got your text. You can't get on that plane. Just . . . whatever you do, do *not* get on that plane. Trust me. I'll explain later. If you get this, call me back."

She hung up.

"That's your big confession!?" Lane blurted. "That's not gonna stop her."

She started dialing on her own phone.

"What're you doing?" Vivi asked.

"I'm calling Izzy's parents," Lane said.

Vivi grabbed Lane's arm. "What? No! We can't tell them.

They're going to freak when they find out Izzy spent all her graduation money on a trip for no reason!"

"Their daughter is about to get on a plane to a foreign country," Lane said, squirming away. "I think they'll care a little more about that."

Vivi released her. "Good point."

The phone rang. And rang. When it picked up, Lane held her breath. "Hi, you've reached the Hunters."

"Dammit!" She closed her phone. "They're not home."

"All right. That's it." Vivi jumped up and grabbed her bag. "Let's go."

"Where are we going?" Lane asked, scrambling after her.

"To the airport," Vivi said. "We have to stop her."

"We're never gonna get there in time," Lane said, pulling her mom's car keys out of her pocket.

Vivi turned around and snatched the keys out of Lane's hand as she shoved through the door. "In your mom's Jag with me driving? I'll have us there in twenty minutes."

Lane thought about protesting. Her mother would lose it if Lane let Vivi drive her Jag. But it didn't matter. This was an emergency.

✳ ✳ ✳

"Izzy, look, I hate to tell you this on your voice mail, but Brandon isn't real," Lane rambled as she ran at least twenty yards behind Vivi down the concourse at Newark Airport. All around her travelers stopped and stared, and she had this overwhelming sense that at any moment she was going to be tackled by airport security, but she hardly cared. "We made him up. The guy that took you to the prom was named Jonathan. I'm really sorry. We just wanted you to get over Shawn. But you can't get on that plane. He's not even gonna be there when you get there because he's not real! Please, Iz, just . . . just call me back!"

She skidded to a stop next to Vivi, heaving for breath. Vivi, for her part, was a bit pink in the cheeks but otherwise fine. The perks of being on the track team, Lane supposed. Maybe she should have stuck with soccer past freshman year, because she really felt like she was about to have a coronary.

"What?" she asked Vivi, who looked flat-out helpless as she stared at a television screen full of flight numbers and departure times.

"We don't even know what airline she's on," Vivi said flatly. "We don't know what gate, what flight number. And you can't even get past security without a ticket. What was I thinking?"

"No," Lane said, desperate. "You can't give up now. We got here, didn't we? And it's . . ." She lifted her phone to look at the time. It read 12:02. "No!" Lane wailed.

"What? What's the matter?" Vivi asked.

"It's after twelve!" Lane shouted, lifting the phone to show her. "She's gone! She's gone, Vivi!"

"No. She can't be. Maybe she missed her flight!" Vivi said hopefully. "Or maybe it's delayed!" Her eyes scanned the screen again.

"What? In this weather!?" Lane flung her arm toward the

window, which was full of nothing but blue sky. "Face it, Vivi. She's gone. Oh my God. Oh my God! How could I have let you talk me into this!?"

"What!?"

"Don't give me that innocent face!" Lane shouted. "This is all your fault!"

"My fault?" Vivi demanded. "We were both in on this one, Lane."

"Oh, please! You knew I didn't want to do this! I tried to beg you to drop it a thousand times. But no-o-o! You've gotta be right. You're such a freaking control . . . freak that you have to make all the decisions in everyone else's lives! Well, look where it's gotten us, Vivi!" Lane shouted, throwing her arms out. "We're in an airport and Isabelle's on a plane to a freaking foreign country!"

"Oh, you are so innocent aren't you?" Vivi countered. "Do I have to remind you that just last night you were all proud of yourself for helping to convince Jonathan to come to the prom after he bailed on me?"

Lane's face stung. She *had* been rather giddy about that at the time—feeling as though she'd maybe done something right where Vivi had screwed up. But that was then—when Isabelle was happily posing for prom pictures. This was now—when Isabelle was watching a stewardess point out emergency exits.

"That is so not the point," Lane said.

"Well, I think it is!" Vivi shouted. "If you and Marshall hadn't talked Jonathan into showing up, we wouldn't be in this mess right now."

236

"If *I* hadn't talked him into showing up!?" Lane exclaimed, incredulous. "You made me do that! I could have been at a party with Curtis that night asking him to the prom, but instead you begged me to fix your problem and I did! It's always about you!"

Vivi's jaw dropped slightly, and Lane felt an instant pang of guilt as her words hung in the air around them. They had started to draw a bit of a crowd, and a few college guys standing nearby ooohed at her dig.

"Oh, really?" Vivi said, stepping closer to Lane. "Well, you didn't *have* to go. It's not like I held a gun to your head. Is the word *no* even in your vocabulary, you pushover?"

"*Oooooh,*" the guys chorused again.

Lane's eyes misted over. Vivi had just hit her where it hurt the most. In front of all these people. At that moment she hated the girl. Hated her more than anything. This *was* her fault. It *was*. And no one was going to convince her otherwise.

"That's it. I'm outta here," Lane said, grabbing the keys from Vivi's hands. She turned and started to storm away.

"Where are you going?" Vivi yelled after her. "You can't leave me here."

"Yes, I can! It's my car!" Lane turned to shout back.

"Lane, you can't be serious," Vivi said.

Lane paused and crossed her arms over her chest. "Fine, Vivi. You want a ride home, you're gonna have to ask me nicely."

Vivi looked around at their audience, the color rising in her cheeks. Clearly she was hating every minute of this.

But there was also no other way out. For once, Lane had the power. "Fine, Lane. Can I please have a ride home?"

"Um, let me think about that," Lane said, bringing a thoughtful finger to her chin. "*No!*"

Then, to the applauding crowd's delight, Lane turned around and stormed toward the automatic sliding doors.

★ ★ twenty-two ★ ★

Lane was so pumped up and petrified at the same time, she felt as if she were losing her mind. Before long she found herself driving down her sun-drenched street, having no idea how she'd gotten there. She had taken her mother's car on the highway—to Newark Airport, no less—and she didn't even remember which roads she'd taken or what exits she'd used.

Probably not a good sign. She hoped she hadn't cut anybody off or caused any accidents. That would be really bad.

The thought of unknowingly leaving a string of wrecks behind her somehow struck her as funny as she approached the corner where Curtis's house sat like a beacon in the sun next to her own.

"I made up a guy. I made up a guy for my best friend and hired someone to pretend he was him and now she's on her way to France to be with him, but he's not there. No, he's not! He's not there because he doesn't exist!"

Lane pulled into her driveway and gasped a few times, trying to get control of herself.

"And I told off my best friend! The only friend I have left! I told her off just for being herself! What kind of person does that? A crazy person, that's who," she said, tears squeezing out the corner of her eyes. "I am a crazy person who is shouting at herself and crying in her mother's car!"

She choked in a few breaths and yanked a tissue out of the box in the center console. She blew her nose loudly and wiped at her eyes.

"And I asked you to the prom!" she shouted at Curtis's house. "Do you have any idea how hard that was?" she cried. "Do you have any freaking clue?"

Just then, Curtis's garage door slid open and out Curtis came, straddling his dirt bike. He looked happy and carefree and adorable in his black cargo shorts and an old, faded concert tee. So happy and carefree and adorable, it sent Lane's pulse racing. Without thinking, she got out of the car and slammed the door. Curtis almost fell off his bike, he was so startled.

"Wow. Give a guy a little warning," he said, righting himself.

Full of sudden fire, Lane stormed across her yard. "I have to tell you something!" she shouted. Almost screeched.

"Okay." Curtis put his bike down in the driveway. He looked freaked, but Lane didn't care. The words were coming and she was not going to stop them.

"When I asked you to the prom that night, I wanted to go with you," she said, standing right in front of him. "I mean,

I *really* wanted to go with you. Not as friends. Not as some last-minute pity date. I wanted to go with you. In fact, I've wanted to go with you forever. And I know that might freak you out, but it's how I feel. And I'm tired of not saying how I feel!"

She stopped and shoved her hands under her arms, clinging to her sweater as her chest heaved up and down. Curtis stared at her.

"So. How do you feel about that?" Lane said, petrified.

"I feel like an idiot," Curtis said, shrugging slightly.

Lane blinked. "Okay."

"No. Not okay," Curtis said. "Lane, I really wanted to go to the prom with you, too. I almost asked you, like, a hundred times, but I kept chickening out. I thought you would laugh in my face."

"No," Lane said.

"Yes!"

"I thought you were gonna laugh in *my* face!" Lane said. "And then you told me there was that girl you were interested in . . ."

"There was a girl I was interested in. You!" Curtis said, throwing his hand out at her. "I only said that to see how you would react and you had no reaction, so I figured . . . you know . . . that you weren't interested. But even then I kept trying to set up, like, situations where I could ask you. Like asking you to pick out a tux with me. I figured that would be the perfect opener, but you said no."

Lane's jaw dropped. "No."

"And then the party. I was going to ask you there. . . ."

"No!"

"You keep saying that," Curtis said with a smirk.

"Well, I don't know what else to say!" Lane blurted. "I thought you were in love with Kim Wolfe or something."

"I only asked her because you bailed on me for the party," Curtis told Lane. "I was going to ask you that night, but when you weren't even home, I just kind of figured you couldn't care less. So I asked the first girl I saw."

"No."

"Yes!"

"So you're not in love with her?" Lane asked, her voice squeaking.

"Not even close," Curtis said with a laugh.

He stepped closer to her. So close, she could count the gold flecks in his eyes. Lane looked at the ground, suddenly shy, but Curtis ducked his head to get back in her line of vision. He was smiling. And before she knew it, his lips touched hers. His hand was on her lower back. His other hand pulled her closer to him. Her heart swooped as she gave in completely. She was kissing Curtis. Curtis was kissing her.

Before she could stop herself, she started to laugh.

"What happened?" Curtis said, his eyes half-closed. "Are you laughing at me?"

"What? No! No. Not at you." Lane was warm and happy and disbelieving. "It's this day. I'm laughing at this day."

"So it wasn't the kiss." Curtis wanted to be sure.

"It wasn't the kiss. I promise. The kiss was good. The kiss was great, actually."

Curtis stood up straight, all proud of himself.

"But I have to go," Lane said, backing away. "Can we do this later?"

The self-satisfaction disappeared from Curtis's face. "Are you serious? We wait this long and now you want to wait longer?"

"I don't want to, but I have to." Lane bit her lip. "I have to go find Vivi and apologize and then I have to go over to Isabelle's house and tell her parents that I shipped their daughter off to a foreign country."

"Pardon?" Curtis said.

"I'll explain later," Lane said. "Bye!"

Curtis lifted a hand in a confused wave and Lane giggled all the way to Vivi's house.

Vivi jogged out of her house with the cash to pay her cab-driver, just as Lane was pulling up along the curb. She was surprised by how relieved she was to see her friend. After Lane's unprecedented freakout in the airport, Vivi had thought there was a good chance she would never see the girl again.

"Thanks for waiting," Vivi told the cabdriver, handing over a good chunk of the money she'd gotten back from Jonathan. Which, she supposed, she actually owed him now. As the cab drove off, Vivi turned to face Lane, who was approaching with a sheepish look on her face.

"You had to take a cab home, huh?" Lane asked, biting her lip.

"Girl's gotta do what a girl's gotta do," Vivi said, pushing her hands into the back pockets of her jeans. "Lane, I'm *so* sorry! I didn't mean to call you a pushover."

Lane smiled. "I didn't mean to say you were a control freak—"

"But I am," Vivi said, lifting her shoulders. "We all know I am."

"Yeah, but it was still a mean way to say it," Lane replied.

Suddenly exhausted, Vivi turned around and dropped down on her front lawn, letting out a groan. "This has already been a really long day."

"No kidding," Lane said, sitting next to her.

Vivi took a deep breath and stared down at the patch of grass between her knees. Her face felt hot and her heart was sick with dread. "I really screwed up this time, didn't I?" she said.

"Well, this *is* the first time one of your schemes has gone intercontinental," Lane joked, squinting one eye against the sun as she looked at Vivi.

Vivi managed to laugh. "I'm really sorry, Lane. For everything. I don't know what I was thinking with this one. I must have been out of my mind."

"Well, don't be too hard on yourself. Somehow in all the insanity I did manage to finally kiss Curtis," Lane said.

Vivi felt like she'd just been spun around like a Tilt-A-Whirl. "You *what*!?"

Lane beamed. "I just went over there. I told him I liked him. He told me he liked me. And we kissed."

"Shut *up!*" Vivi said, shoving Lane over with both hands. Lane braced herself with her elbow to the ground and laughed. "I knew it! I knew he liked you back!"

"Appears that way." Lane blushed like crazy.

"How was it?" Vivi demanded, turning to face her.

"Amazing. Perfect. Everything I always wanted," Lane confirmed, her blue eyes shining.

For the first time in days, Vivi's heart felt full. It didn't feel jealous or guilty or nervous—just full of happiness for her friend.

"Lane, I am *so* happy for you," she said, reaching over to hug her.

"Me too," Lane said.

When they pulled back again, Lane picked at a blade of grass near her hip. "I just wish it could have turned out the same way for you and Jonathan."

Vivi sighed as her chest constricted once again. "Well, that was never meant to be."

"Are you sure?" Lane asked. "Maybe if you called him?"

Just like that, Vivi's tension was back full force. "Maybe, but we have bigger problems to deal with right now."

"Right," Lane said, looking across the street. "Guess I was trying not to think about that."

"Come on." Vivi shoved herself up and then yanked Lane to her feet by her wrist. "Let's go inside and figure out what to do next."

Lane took a deep breath and blew it out. "Sounds like a plan."

As they walked into the house, Vivi tried to look at the

bright side. At least she still had Lane. At least she wasn't in this entirely alone. No matter how forlorn her heart felt.

✶ ✶ ✶

Several hours and much procrastination later, Vivi and Lane stood before the red front door at Isabelle's house, unable to move. Every time Vivi even thought about raising her finger to ring the doorbell, her resolve left her.

"Maybe we don't really need to do this," she said. "They have to know, right? Isabelle's not an idiot. She'd tell her parents if she was getting on a plane."

"We can't assume that," Lane said firmly, sounding as if she was trying to convince herself as much as Vivi. "We have to find out."

"Why hasn't she called yet?" Vivi looked at her phone. She and Lane had calculated it out. If Isabelle's flight really left at noon, she'd be in Paris by now. This whole thing would be so much easier if Vivi could tell Izzy's mom that she'd heard from her and she was okay. "Maybe we should just wait until she calls."

"Enough stalling," Lane said.

With that, Lane lifted her hand and rang the bell. Vivi's stomach dropped out of her body.

"What are you doing?" Vivi blurted.

"Biting the bullet," Lane said.

Vivi closed her eyes, feeling as if she were cresting the top of the highest hill on a roller coaster. Her heart was in her throat. Her stomach was where her heart should have been. And suddenly she had to pee like she'd never had to pee before. She heard footsteps. Heard the doorknob turning. This was it. There was no turning back.

"Well, hello, girls!" Isabelle's mother was a vision of calm, unperturbed ignorance—all pearls and pressed cotton and perfect teeth. So she didn't know. She didn't know a thing. Vivi looked at Lane. Lane looked like she was about to bolt. Vivi grabbed her hand.

"Hi, Mrs. Hunter," she choked out.

"Come in! Come in!" Mrs. Hunter trilled, opening the door wide.

Vivi could feel Lane shaking as they stepped inside. She felt like a prisoner being walked out in front of the firing squad. What was Mrs. Hunter going to do when she found out? Was she going to scream? Throw things? Faint? Were they going to have to call 911?

"Isabelle's not home right now, but you're welcome to wait for her in her room," Isabelle's mother said.

That could be a long wait, Vivi thought.

"Actually, Mrs. Hunter, there's something we have to tell you," Vivi began, hoping against hope that this wouldn't be as bad as she was imagining.

"What's that, hon?" Isabelle's mother asked with a smile.

Vivi looked at Lane. Lane stared at Vivi. There was no air in the room. No turning back. And suddenly, Vivi heard the words spilling from her lips.

"We didn't mean to do it, Mrs. Hunter! Honestly! We were just trying to help!" Vivi blurted.

"Didn't mean to do what, Vivi?" Mrs. Hunter asked, nonplussed. "What's the matter?"

"It's Isabelle," Lane said. "And Brandon. You remember Brandon, right? From last night?"

Mrs. Hunter crossed her arms over her chest. Her expression grew concerned. "Yes . . ."

"He's not real!" Vivi blurted. "We made him up!"

"On MySpace. We made him up on MySpace to help Izzy get over Shawn," Lane said.

"We gave him a dog and drums and books and movies," Vivi rambled.

"And then we had Marshall IM her, pretending to be him—"

"All we wanted was to get Izzy over Shawn! That was it! But then she wanted to go to the prom with Shawn, so—"

"So we had Marshall ask her. Well, Brandon. Well, Marshall as Brandon," Lane rambled. "But then we had to actually *have* a Brandon—"

"So we hired one," Vivi said, swallowing hard. "We hired a guy from Cranston Prep and he was totally hot, right? Wasn't he hot?"

Mrs. Hunter gaped at her.

"So not the point, Vivi," Lane said through her teeth.

"Right, sorry," Vivi said, chagrined.

"Girls, as appalled as I am right now, I'm getting the idea that you haven't gotten to the point." Mrs. Hunter nervously fiddled with her pearls.

"Well, we had Jonathan—that's the guy who pretended to be Brandon—we had him break up with her last night and say he was going to Paris," Lane said. "We figured it was foolproof, you know? No one wants a long-distance relationship at eighteen, right? But the problem is . . . the problem is . . ."

Vivi took a deep breath and closed her eyes. The words all came out in one quick rush. "The problem is that Izzy is on a flight to Paris right now to find him!"

"What!?" Mrs. Hunter screeched.

"Except he's not there! He doesn't even exist!" Vivi couldn't stop herself. "Izzy used all her graduation money to chase after a guy who we made up!"

"Mrs. Hunter we are so, so, *so* sorry," Lane said tremulously.

"How could you *do* this?" Mrs. Hunter raved. "She's on a plane? Right now? To *Paris*!?"

"Mrs. Hunter—"

"Don't even speak to me, Vivi Swayne," Mrs. Hunter snapped, slicing a finger through the air.

Vivi pulled back, feeling as if she'd been slapped. The lump in her throat grew. "I'm sorry."

"Oh my gosh! My baby!" Mrs. Hunter covered her mouth with her hands, her eyes wide. "She's going to be all alone in a foreign country!" She turned around and rushed into the kitchen. After the briefest hesitation, Vivi and Lane followed. Mrs. Hunter grabbed her purse and keys and looked around in a panic. "My passport! I need my passport!"

"Mrs. Hunter, what are you doing?" Lane asked.

"I have to go after her! She's going to be all alone!" Mrs. Hunter rambled. "I have to find my passport." She turned again and swept past them, running up the stairs in her sensible heels.

Vivi stood in the foyer, gripping the banister, feeling hollow. She could hardly breathe. "Omigod, she hates us," she said, holding her hand over her chest. "Could this possibly get any worse?"

Suddenly, Vivi's cell phone rang. She pulled it out, shaking like a leaf, and saw Isabelle's name on the caller ID. "It's her!"

Lane gasped and huddled in to hear.

"Izzy!" Vivi shouted into the phone, barely able to grip it in her quaking hands. "Are you okay? What were you thinking? Your mother is freaking out right now. She's on her way to Paris to get you!"

Total silence.

"Iz? Are you there?" Vivi wailed in desperation. "Where *are* you?"

And then, a hand came down on her shoulder. Vivi whirled around, and Isabelle was standing right in front of her.

✭ ✭ twenty-three ✭ ✭

"What . . . what . . . what?" Vivi could not get past that one word.

"Izzy! You're here!" Lane threw her arms around Isabelle's neck.

"I can't believe you losers actually thought I'd follow some guy I barely know to France," Isabelle said, smiling at Vivi over Lane's shoulder. She was wearing a bathing suit and terry cloth shorts, glistening like she'd been out in the sun all day.

"But . . . but . . . I—"

Isabelle pulled away from Lane, lifted her phone, and snapped a picture of Vivi's face. "Nice. I really had to get that one for posterity."

"Isabelle," Vivi said finally. "What is going on?"

"Why don't you come out back and see?" Isabelle said, tilting her head toward the back of the house.

Vivi looked at Lane as they followed Isabelle through the kitchen to the back patio. Lane looked as baffled as Vivi felt. Baffled and relieved. Isabelle stepped outside.

"They're here!" she sang.

Confused, Vivi walked out into the glare of the sun. For a second she was blinded, but she could make out two figures sitting in lounge chairs alongside the shimmering pool. Two shadowy figures that ever-so-slowly came into focus.

Marshall kicked back, sipping an iced tea in distressed khaki shorts and a cool T-shirt, and Jonathan looking as Abercrombie-perfect as ever in a polo and linen pants. He was all clean-shaven now, his hair back to its preppy flatness instead of the tousled Brandon effect.

"Ladies!" Jonathan said with a grin. "How was Newark Airport?"

Vivi couldn't move. Could hardly process what she was seeing. Even in all her confusion, Vivi was ecstatic just to see him again.

"You remember Jonathan, right? He never really looked like a Brandon to me," Isabelle said with a shrug. "But then I guess he never was a Brandon!"

"How long have you known?" Vivi asked finally.

"Since last weekend. The night of our first 'date,'" Isabelle gloated, throwing in some air quotes.

"So this whole week . . . this whole week with you crying and moping and everything. It was all a sham," Lane said.

"Yep. Who knew I was such a good actress?" Isabelle preened. "And my mom did a great job just now, didn't she? Maybe she should audition for your mom's next show, Viv!"

"I think I need to sit down," Vivi said, dropping into a chair at the table. She couldn't believe it. She'd been outplayed. By Isabelle, of all people—the least deceitful person she knew.

"It was hard, believe me," Isabelle replied, sitting as well. "I *so* wanted to tell you that I knew. But it was way more fun to mess with your heads."

"But . . . but how?" Vivi asked.

"Brandon and I . . . well, *Marshall* and I were chatting online that night after our date and I asked him if he wanted to go so he could go to bed early," Isabelle replied, smiling. "And he told me that he'd slept like a rock the night before so he could stay up all night talking to me if I wanted. Which was sweet, but clearly a lie. Since on our date, *Jonathan* had told me that he had been up until four in the morning playing his guitar."

Vivi shot eye-daggers at Marshall, who sank down in his chair a bit and covered his eyes with his sunglasses.

"So after some IM grilling, I finally got his true identity out of him and he spilled about—what did you call it?—Operation Skewer Sluttig?"

Vivi winced. "Yeah."

"Spilled the whole can o' beans," Isabelle continued. "That was when I decided to come up with my own plot."

"So she called you," Lane said to Jonathan.

"Yep. There was a message from Izzy when I got home from my friend's house that night. Marshall got her my number and she called me and told me she knew everything and that she had a plan to get back at you," Jonathan said. "And

I don't know, but for some reason at that very moment, getting back at you seemed like an attractive idea," he added, smirking at Vivi.

Vivi's heart was spasming like crazy. *What does this mean?* She wanted to scream. *Was all that mushy stuff between you and Izzy last night just to get back at me? Or did you actually fall in love with each other while plotting your revenge?*

"Omigod! The look on your faces when I told you I thought he was going to say he loved me?" Isabelle said, cracking up. "That was so classic! I *wish* I'd gotten a picture of *that.*"

"So you're not mad?" Lane asked.

"Not anymore. I was at first. I mean, I was like Count of Monte Cristo mad," Isabelle said. "But after I talked to Jonathan and Marshall about it, it sounded like your hearts were in the right places. I mean, who else has friends that would go so overboard just to make their friend happy?"

"I cannot believe you made us think you were going to Paris," Vivi said, laughing as she rolled her eyes. "That was so not cool."

"Yeah, and making me believe I had a brand-new dream guy just to keep me away from Shawn? Not cool either," Isabelle said sternly. She stood up and walked over to Vivi and Lane. "You guys, you don't have to protect me, okay? I can take care of myself."

Vivi sat up straight. "But I—"

"You have got to learn to keep your mouth shut," Isabelle said firmly.

Vivi snapped her mouth closed.

"And you!" Isabelle turned abruptly to Lane with her arms crossed over her chest. "You cannot tell me you thought this was a good idea."

Lane looked at Vivi. "I . . . well . . . no."

"Well, God, girl! Speak up! If you would just learn to stand up for yourself already, we could have avoided this whole thing!" Isabelle teased.

"Oh, she learned to stand up for herself, believe me," Vivi said proudly.

"Yeah?" Isabelle raised her eyebrows.

"I kind of left her at the airport," Lane said with a shrug.

"No way," Isabelle said, her jaw dropping.

"Yep." Lane preened.

"Wow. Nice," Isabelle said, slapping hands with Lane. "You'll have to tell me all about that later."

"I guess I deserved that one." Vivi shook her head, smiling. "I'm really sorry, Izzy. It all went very wrong."

Isabelle smiled slowly. "Well, not *totally* wrong," she said. "Thanks to you guys, I finally found someone who cares about me." She slowly walked around the table toward the lounge chairs. "Someone who really listens to me and treats me the way I deserve to be treated."

Vivi's heart pounded in her throat. Oh, God. So it was true. Isabelle and Jonathan really *had* fallen for each other. She could only imagine all the late-night phone calls they must have had, putting together their plans. All the whispering and scheming. So all that stuff at the prom—the touching and gooey eyes and lap sitting—it was all real. Vivi was going to die. Right here, right now.

"My perfect guy," Isabelle said, pausing between the two chairs.

And then, Marshall stood up, took Isabelle in his arms, and kissed her like there was no tomorrow.

"Marshall!" Vivi blurted.

"No! Isabelle! You can't date Marshall! He's gay!" Lane shouted.

"What!?" Vivi cried. She brought her hands to her head. "Okay. Is this what an aneurysm feels like?"

Marshall pulled away from Isabelle and laughed. "Lane, I'm not gay. I was just messing with you. You caught me staring at her and I had to throw you off, so I said I liked Jonathan."

"I'm so going to hurl," Vivi said.

Isabelle laughed and hugged Marshall and they kissed again.

"Ew. Okay. I cannot watch this," Vivi rambled. "What is wrong with you people? I did *not* sign off on this!"

"Vivi," Jonathan said, pushing himself out of his chair.

"I mean, Isabelle and Marshall? This cannot happen," Vivi continued.

Jonathan walked over and stood in front of her. "Vivi!"

"What?" she blurted.

"Would you shut up already?" he said.

Vivi's mouth snapped shut. Jonathan's blue eyes sparkled as he looked at her. "What did you just say to me?" she asked.

"I said, 'shut up,'" he told her. Then he reached out, grabbed her by the waist, and pulled her to him. Vivi gasped in surprise, and then he kissed her. He kissed until she was floating somewhere outside herself—letting everything go.

When he finally pulled away, all she wanted was to pull him back again.

"Okay! Feeling very fifth wheel out here!" Lane said with a laugh. She turned and headed inside. "I'll just be getting a drink!"

"So I didn't scare you away?" Vivi asked Jonathan.

Jonathan took a step back, but held on to her hand. "Takes a lot more than one freak-out in a parking lot to scare me off," he said with a manly shrug. "Just took me a couple of days to realize it."

"A couple of days? Try a week!"

"Well, a guy has to play hard to get . . . ," he teased.

"You suck, you know that?"

"No, you suck."

"No, it's definitely you. You definitely, definitely—"

"Okay, this could go on for days. I have a better idea," Jonathan said.

Then he pulled her to him once more, and this time neither one of them was about to let go.

★ ★ twenty-four ★ ★

A few weeks later, Vivi sat in the sun with the rest of her class in her white cap and gown, smiling at Jonathan in the first row of the bleachers. Next to her, Lane and Curtis clutched hands. Up on the makeshift stage in the middle of the Westmont High football field, Isabelle was just finishing up her valedictorian speech. Vivi felt nothing but excited and accomplished and proud. She was having a perfect moment.

"Congratulations to the graduating class of Westmont High!" Isabelle shouted.

Vivi jumped to her feet and cheered with the rest of the class, throwing her cap into the air. Hundreds of white and black disks sailed up into the cloudless blue sky. And then came back down again.

"Duck!" Curtis shouted. And they all did.

"Ow!" Vivi said with a laugh as a hard corner slammed right into her back.

"That tradition has got to go," Lane replied, shaking her head.

"You guys! We graduated!" Vivi shouted. She grabbed them into a group hug as everyone around them high-fived and snapped pictures.

"We are officially OOS!" Curtis cheered.

"Huh?" Vivi asked.

"Out of school!" Curtis explained with a grin.

"Yeah, and now that we're OOS, maybe it's really time for you to quit that crap already," Vivi said.

"Bite me, Vivi," Curtis replied.

"Not BM?" Vivi shot back.

Curtis chuckled. "You said BM!"

"You guys?" Lane said.

"You are such a . . . a . . . guy!" Vivi countered.

"Hey! You finally noticed!" Curtis replied. "Congrats."

"You guys!" Lane shouted.

"What?" Vivi asked.

"Where's Isabelle?" Lane peered around through the mayhem. Parents and friends had started to crowd the field to take pictures with the graduates. "We need to get a picture. She was supposed to come right down here."

"I don't know," Vivi said, looking around. "She probably just got snagged by some people wanting a picture of the valedictorian."

Jonathan arrived and planted a big kiss on Vivi's cheek. "Congratulations!" he said, handing her a big bouquet of roses.

"Thanks," Vivi said, beaming. "But where's my real present?"

"What's that?" Jonathan teased.

"You promised! You promised you were going to tell me the story of the scar!" Vivi cried. "So come on. Give it. Spill!"

"Okay, fine, fine." Jonathan turned her toward him, wrapping one arm around her waist. "I got this scar," he said, leaning in close as if he was going to tell her a dark, tragic secret. "Trying to jump a ramp on my tricycle when I was four."

"No way!" Vivi said with a laugh.

"I told you I could be badass," he said with a blithe shrug.

Vivi laughed and stood on her toes to kiss him. "That's the cutest, most pathetic thing I've ever heard."

"Tell me about it," he said with a grin.

"Okay, where is Isabelle?" Lane asked, growing frustrated.

Suddenly, Vivi's cell phone beeped. She lifted her gown and fished under the folds of fabric until she could get to the pocket of her shorts. When she pulled it out, the text message icon was flashing on the screen.

"It's from her. What the heck?" Vivi said.

Lane, Curtis, and Jonathan all huddled around her as she read.

Isabelle: Guess where I am. And no. Not with Shawn.
Vivi: Ha ha. Better not B! U break M's heart.
Isabelle: Im @ Newark Airport

"She's hilarious. Really," Curtis deadpanned.

Vivi: V. FUNNY!

> **Isabelle:** OK. Not there yet. But our flight leaves in 4 hrs. U,
> me, Lane going 2 paris. Go home and pack!!! HAPPY GRADUATION!

"What?" Vivi blurted.

"Yeah, what? What about me?" Curtis put in.

"She can't be serious." Lane grabbed the phone from Vivi.

"Hey! That's my phone!" Vivi protested.

"Back off, Vivi!" Lane replied.

"Wow. She's getting good at this," Jonathan gave Vivi a squeeze as Lane texted back. Vivi smiled. She was actually fairly proud of Lane's newfound guts.

> **Vivi:** its lane. r u serious?
> **Isabelle:** TOTALLY SERIOUS! Remember grad $$$? Now GO!
> Meet at my house 1 hr.! Don't 4get yr passports!!

Lane closed the phone and looked at Vivi, dumbfounded. "We're going to Paris."

Vivi's heart skipped with excitement. "We're going to Paris!"

She grabbed Lane's hand and they jumped up and down, squealing happily. "Come on! Let's go pack!" Lane exclaimed, squeezing Vivi's fingers as they started navigating through the crowd.

"Uh, ladies!?" Jonathan called after them, clearing his throat.

Vivi and Lane turned around. Jonathan and Curtis were staring after them forlornly. "Yes?"

"What about us?" Curtis asked, lifting his palms.

Vivi looked at Lane and grinned. "Well, you'll just have to pine for us until we get back," Lane shouted.

"Unless, of course, you want to hop a plane and follow us, but that's your prerogative!" Vivi added. "I'm done telling people what to do."

And with that, she and Lane jogged off, hand in hand, to go get Izzy.

acknowledgments

Special thanks to Katie McConnaughey, Emily Meehan, Josh Bank, Lynn Weingarten, and Courtney Bongiolatti for their patience and help in guiding this novel. You all know I couldn't have done it without you!